What They Have

by Kate Robin

A SAMUEL FRENCH ACTING EDITION

SAMUEL FRENCH

FOUNDED 1830

NEW YORK HOLLYWOOD LONDON TORONTO

SAMUELFRENCH.COM

ISBN 978-0-573-66376-5   Printed in U.S.A.   #25759

MUSIC USE NOTE

Licensees are solely responsible for obtaining formal written permission from copyright owners to use copyrighted music in the performance of this play and are strongly cautioned to do so. If no such permission is obtained by the licensee, then the licensee must use only original music that the licensee owns and controls. Licensees are solely responsible and liable for all music clearances and shall indemnify the copyright owners of the play and their licensing agent, Samuel French, Inc., against any costs, expenses, losses and liabilities arising from the use of music by licensees.

IMPORTANT BILLING AND CREDIT REQUIREMENTS

All producers of *WHAT THEY HAVE must* give credit to the Author of the Play in all programs distributed in connection with performances of the Play, and in all instances in which the title of the Play appears for the purposes of advertising, publicizing or otherwise exploiting the Play and/or a production. The name of the Author *must* appear on a separate line on which no other name appears, immediately following the title and *must* appear in size of type not less than fifty percent of the size of the title type.

In addition, the following credit *must* appear in all programs and publicity material distributed in association with the Play:

Commissioned and First Produced by
South Coast Repertory, Costa Mesa, CA

WHAT THEY HAVE had its world premiere on April 4th, 2008 at South Coast Repertory, David Emmes, Producing Artistic Director, Martin Benson, Artistic Director, Paula Tomei, Managing Director. The production was directed by Chris Fields with the following creative staff and cast:

Scenic Designer: Christopher Barreca
Costume Designer: Alex Jaeger
Lighting Designer: Lap-Chi Chu
Original Music/Musical Director: Michael Roth
Dramaturg: Megan Monaghan

Cast (in alphabetical order):

SUZANNE . . . . Nancy Bell
CONNIE . . . . Marin Hinkle
JONAS . . . . Matt Letscher
MATT . . . . Kevin Rahm

CHARACTERS

CONNIE. very late 30's
JONAS. a little older
SUZANNE. very late 30's
MATT. a little younger
DR. COSTIGAN. actor playing Matt
ANESTHESIOLOGIST. actress playing Suzanne
DR. MORSE. actor playing Jonas
GENEVA. actress playing Suzanne
ALLAN KOZAN KATZ. actor playing Matt

PLACE

Los Angeles

TIME

Early summer 2007 - Late summer 2008

Scene One

(Suzanne's studio: A converted garage filled with sensual abstract landscape paintings.)

*(***CONNIE****, four months pregnant, sips a ginger ale,* ***JONAS*** *holds a beer, and* ***MATT*** *eats cashews. They watch intently as* ***SUZANNE*** *moves a canvas to reveal a red on red painting.)*

CONNIE. Beautiful.

SUZANNE. Thanks.

CONNIE. Jonas?

JONAS. Love it.

CONNIE. We may have to buy this one too. Do we have room?

JONAS. Done. Sold.

CONNIE. But where?

JONAS. We'll find a place.

CONNIE. But the red...? Will the blue work better with what we have?

JONAS. Either way. I love them both.

SUZANNE. I love these two also. The red, especially, is a personal favorite.

CONNIE. Hm. *(pause)* It's so...it's very haunting really. Almost violent and peaceful at the same time. That's inane, isn't it?

SUZANNE. I know what you mean.

CONNIE. I mean, like, after the battle. Like a battlefield after it's all over – that pre-dawn of futility – the kind of peace you're desperate for – thirst – the thirst for peace or the...what's the word – craving?

JONAS. Rebuke.

CONNIE. Oh my god, yes! The silent rebuke of a bloody peace.

SUZANNE. There's a title.

MATT. How is "rebuke" a word for "craving?"

JONAS. It's not.

CONNIE. It's as if the peace was always there but there had to be bloodshed to get to it. I mean, God, it's profound, because of the *humanity. (She belches.)* Oh, I think I have to go puke…

(MATT grabs a garbage can and holds it under CONNIE's face. CONNIE shakes her head and runs out of the room. SUZANNE calls after her.)

SUZANNE. You need some more soda?

MATT. I'll get her some.

(MATT follows CONNIE. Disturbed, SUZANNE watches them go.)

JONAS. She's fine.

(silence)

JONAS. It really is lovely.

SUZANNE. Thank you. *(pause)* How's the show?

JONAS. Good. Great. You know.

SUZANNE. Sure. Great. I mean, it's a huge success.

(pause)

JONAS. You don't watch it, do you?

SUZANNE. We try to see it, but you know we don't have a TV.

JONAS. Right.

SUZANNE. Matt can't have one in the house. It saps his creativity.

JONAS. Just having it there.

SUZANNE. He can't turn it off. If it's there. It consumes him. Like an addiction.

JONAS. You can just say you don't like the show.

SUZANNE. No! It's really smart. My sister loves it!

JONAS. It's not really. There's a lot of...compromise. It's commercial.

SUZANNE. Right. I know what you mean. *(pause)* It's that way for me, too.

JONAS. It is?

SUZANNE. With commissioned work – you know, some of them – certain series, really appeal to the corporate buyers- like for offices or hotels...

JONAS. I thought I saw one of your seascapes at the bank –

SUZANNE. Bank of America?

JONAS. On Sunset.

SUZANNE. Yeah!

JONAS. It looked great.

SUZANNE. Thanks. So, yeah, the dealer always wants more of that kind of thing and they're easy- I mean, I know how to make them, there's no surprises, and we need to eat, you know.... But then there's less time to find something new – something less...understood, you know?

JONAS. Exactly.

SUZANNE. But it is different. I mean, no one knows who I am – I'm barely making a living.

JONAS. Making a living is overrated. As long as you can eat. It's better to be doing what you love, than...I don't know, redecorating.

SUZANNE. You're doing what you love.

JONAS. Yeah. I mean, I have ways of living with myself.

SUZANNE. What do you mean?

JONAS. Just, you know, you're so limited by the networks, in terms of what you can do and how you can do it. They really need everything to be very...accessible, at all times.

SUZANNE. Right.

JONAS. But I always find ways to sneak in something that really matters to me. I mean, the whole show is a metaphor for me, about living in a post-moral universe.

SUZANNE. Hm.

JONAS. Which, I think, some viewers understand. On some level. I mean, I like to believe it's an element of why people watch. And not just because the actors are incredibly hot.

SUZANNE. I'm sure it is. *(pause)* Do you still work on your novels at all?

JONAS. Not really. Not much.

SUZANNE. Why not take some time off then? Just focus on that.

JONAS. I can't take the failure. For the moment. And now, with the baby coming…I need to milk my prime earning years for all they're worth.

SUZANNE. Hm.

JONAS. But I think you're just as successful as I am. If not more so.

SUZANNE. I don't think most people would agree with you.

JONAS. They would if they saw this painting.

SUZANNE. But they won't. *(pause)* "The Silent Rebuke of a Bloody Peace?"

JONAS. She's good with a title.

SUZANNE. Well, thanks.

JONAS. It's personal. It's revealing. I'm not even sure I can still do that. *(pause)* I can buy it. So there's that.

SUZANNE. There is that.

(SUZANNE *sighs.*)

JONAS. Is Matt…? What's Matt up to?

SUZANNE. Teaching. You know, he teaches guitar in the public schools now.

JONAS. Right. I did know that. How's he liking it?

SUZANNE. Well…he likes the fact that it makes him feel like a good person – I don't mean that, that way.

JONAS. I know what you mean –

SUZANNE. I mean, he likes the fact –

JONAS. That he's doing something good

SUZANNE. Yes. Being part of the solution.

JONAS. Of course. It's great.

SUZANNE. It is great. *(pause)* It's not, you know, Music.

JONAS. It is music.

SUZANNE. It's not being a musician. You know –

JONAS. – Right.

SUZANNE. – recording and performing. It's not that.

JONAS. No. It's not. That.

SUZANNE. It's like that.

JONAS. But not.

SUZANNE. Right. But it's a really fun, really wonderful job.

(MATT enters with a plate of mushroom caps.)

MATT. Mushroom cap?

SUZANNE. Thank you.

(JONAS and SUZANNE each pop a cap in their mouths.)

MATT. Stuffed with lamb.

SUZANNE. Delicious.

(JONAS delicately spits his cap into his hand.)

JONAS. Excuse me.

MATT. Not good?

SUZANNE. Oh! Jonas doesn't eat meat!

MATT. Sorry, man…

JONAS. No, that's okay. I'm sorry to be rude.

SUZANNE. Is it a health thing? Or compassion?

JONAS. Neither. Both. I don't know. I guess I started feeling weird about pretending there wasn't a murder involved in my meal.

SUZANNE. *(chewing)* I know. I hate myself.

MATT. It never bothers me. I don't know why. It's just nature.

SUZANNE. Some people are just naturally more carnivorous.

MATT. Right, and then we all come up with some philosophical justification for what's just our natural preference.

SUZANNE. Isn't that true of everything we do? Aren't all our ethics just elaborate justifications for our preferences?

MATT. Then why is it so hard for so many people to be good?

JONAS. People who want to be good are good, or at least they think they are. And the ones who "find it hard to be good" don't really want to be good. And they think no one else does either.

(CONNIE comes in, red-nosed.)

CONNIE. Whew!

SUZANNE. Did you get some – ?

(CONNIE holds up her glass. MATT holds up the plate of mushroom caps.)

MATT. Mushroom cap?

(A wave of nausea hits CONNIE. She turns away.)

No?

CONNIE. Sorry. Mushrooms make me gag. I used to love them – before the alien occupation –

MATT. The what?

JONAS. The pregnancy.

MATT. Oh.

CONNIE. Aversions. The only thing I can eat is cheese.

SUZANNE. I wish you'd told us, we made pasta –

CONNIE. Pasta is fine. Anything that makes me fat, I want. Nice healthy things like salads, like I ate when I was a normal person – these make me wretch. And vomiting arugula is not an experience I recommend.

(pause)

Sorry. Was that too gross?

SUZANNE. No.

MATT. Yes.

(silence)

JONAS. Are you guys watching Big Brother? Top Chef?

SUZANNE. We don't have a TV.

JONAS. Oh right! Sorry. It's so hard to accept.

MATT. You watch reality TV?

JONAS. Love it.

MATT. But you're a writer.

JONAS. I know. I finally have something to watch!

CONNIE. He hasn't been this excited about TV since the Anita Hill hearings.

JONAS. You should get a TV. Just for Big Brother.

MATT. The one with all the crazy fake boob people living in a house?

JONAS. We live for it.

SUZANNE. You don't.

CONNIE. We do. It's true.

SUZANNE. Why?

JONAS. Because even though it's...

CONNIE. Self-conscious.

JONAS. No. Even though there's artifice – the emotions are so much more visceral than what they're giving us everywhere else.

CONNIE. On other TV shows –

JONAS. And movies. It's all so fake –

CONNIE. Well, not *all* movies.

JONAS. All movies except Connie's movies, of course.

MATT. The movies she produces.

JONAS. Her movies, yes.

MATT. They're not really *hers.*

JONAS. She gets the Oscar.

CONNIE. God willing.

MATT. You may get the Oscar but someone else directed them –

SUZANNE. Matt, she gets them made. Why are you – ?

MATT. Getting something made isn't the same thing as *making* it.

CONNIE. It really is.

JONAS. Anyway, when Reality is good – when the people are interesting, they have this…

CONNIE. *Authenticity.*

JONAS. No. This emotional *investment* that taps into very basic human needs, like, like…

CONNIE. To win.

JONAS. No. To love! To be chosen! To live happily ever after! They're so human in their…

CONNIE. Longing.

JONAS. No, well, sort of, their…*desire* is so strong –

CONNIE. Longing and desire are the same thing –

JONAS. – it allows their true selves to be revealed.

CONNIE. It's *drama.* Need. Conflict. Transformation! All in one house! Or one island. Or one…boat. It's Aristotelian, really.

JONAS. When Jen cried because they had a bad picture of her on the wall of the Big Brother house –

CONNIE. It wasn't even a bad picture!

JONAS. It was so *real,* such a stark portrait of –

CONNIE. Vanity –

JONAS. No, of –

CONNIE. I know, not vanity –

JONAS. Self-loathing –

CONNIE. Vanity, self-loathing, it's the same really –

JONAS. Just this tragic image of body-identification –

CONNIE. And dysmorphia.

JONAS. How lost we are, as a culture.

CONNIE. What it is to be a woman today –

JONAS. Not just a woman, a person –

CONNIE. What the value system can do, does do to the psyche –

JONAS. It was chilling. It was powerful.

MATT. It was gross.

CONNIE. So you saw it?

JONAS. I thought you didn't have a TV.

MATT. I did happen to see a little of that episode.

SUZANNE. You did?

MATT. Just that scene. I was at the gym. I'm sorry, those people are just fame seeking narcissists.

JONAS. Right! Even the ones where they obviously all just want to be on-camera personalities –

CONNIE. And doesn't everyone, ultimately? Today?

MATT & SUZANNE. No.

JONAS. It just elucidates those moments in your life when your...

CONNIE. Id.

JONAS. No, your need for acknowledgement overpowers your...

CONNIE. Super-ego.

JONAS. No, your dignity, I guess. And, I have to say, there was another moment this year when Jameka was praying to God so –

CONNIE. Insanely!

JONAS. Devoutly, I was going to say –

CONNIE. She was practically speaking in tongues. Begging for God's forgiveness, for the stupidest thing –

JONAS. She gave up her right to compete for Head of Household for five weeks. It was a big deal.

CONNIE. Like God cares.

JONAS. And Jen kept passing by the camera wearing this bunny suit, asking if it made her look fat!

CONNIE. The layers!

JONAS. It was like Beckett.

MATT. Come on.

JONAS. It was closer to Beckett than anything I've seen on stage, maybe ever.

(*MATT and* **SUZANNE** *stare.*)

SUZANNE. Wow.

(**SUZANNE** *eats a mushroom cap.*)

MATT. Reality TV, to me, is further proof that the world is spiraling to a horrible end.

JONAS. Really? I find it hopeful, actually. That people still want to see the truth in some way.

MATT. Truth? It's all totally fake –

JONAS. It's not though. The emotions are so much more raw than those insipid family dramas where everyone looks like they live inside a Pottery Barn catalogue.

CONNIE. When Shandi cried on the phone with her boyfriend she had just betrayed by sleeping with an Italian model, it was one of those moments you never forget.

JONAS. Top Model, season two.

CONNIE. It was operatic. It was.

JONAS. It was real. Her flaws. Her complexity. She didn't have to be some network idiot's idea of "good" to be likeable.

CONNIE. Or some macho cable executive's idea of an edgy anti-hero –

JONAS. An outlaw in the suburbs. God, I'm so bored of that lie. That these sociopaths are heroic because they're not…educated.

CONNIE. Like anyone who's not totally destitute is an idiot who deserves to be robbed and murdered.

SUZANNE. Wait. What?

JONAS. All these shows about mafiosas or drug dealers, or, I don't know, bigamist serial killers, that valorize these sick, vicious criminals and celebrate the victimization of people who are just trying to play by the rules –

CONNIE. Well, it's hip to identify with the criminal.

MATT. Because we *are* all criminals –

CONNIE. God, remember when being counter-culture was actually about something other than validating greed?

SUZANNE. We're not all criminals!

MATT. We all have these dark impulses.

SUZANNE. Matt thinks we're all born evil so we need these moral codes, ethics and all of that, to help us to be good.

CONNIE. That's what Jonas thinks too –

JONAS. No. That's not accurate.

CONNIE. It's not?

JONAS. I think we're born with a capacity for both good-ness and evil and that we look for guidance toward accessing our highest selves –

CONNIE. Well I was close. I believe people are basically good, and then get corrupted by society. *(to* **SUZANNE***)* What do you think, Suze?

MATT. People are definitely born evil. I mean, look at kids. They're vicious.

CONNIE. Not as infants.

MATT. As infants, they're narcissists, totally selfish.

SUZANNE. They're just babies, they're defenseless!

MATT. We go from these greedy grasping need machines to what? Terrible toddlers, tantrums, you can't play with my doll –

SUZANNE. Or my gun. My truck.

MATT. My toy, whatever, to, what's next? "Look at me Mommy!" That lasts a while. And then you're at that horrible age when you're locking the weak kid in the bathroom stall at school, taunting the boy with the weird smell, yanking down little Susie's panties –

SUZANNE. Little Susie?

MATT. Not you, but –

CONNIE. It was an unfortunate name choice.

SUZANNE. This is all very disturbing –

MATT. Then bang you're a snotty adolescent jerking off in the closet, stealing cash from your parents, doing huge amounts of drugs and paying other kids to do your homework. College, more of the same, and then you're an adult: scared, status-seeking, struggling to make it with a ferocious Darwinian drive to get food, shelter and procreate better and faster than the next guy and that's pretty much your life until you die.

(pause)

SUZANNE. Okay…

CONNIE. How much of that was autobiographical?

MATT. All of it. But it was biographical too. About you and all of us.

CONNIE. Anthropological, you mean.

MATT. I guess.

JONAS. Sociological, really.

SUZANNE. Whatever. It was scary, honey.

MATT. Well your naivete can be scary too, sweetie.

SUZANNE. I'm not naive! I grew up in New York!

CONNIE. People who grew up in New York are the most naive.

SUZANNE. What do you mean? You grew up in New York.

CONNIE. I'm terribly naive.

MATT. Please.

JONAS. You're really not.

CONNIE. I am. I always want to believe the best about people.

SUZANNE. What does that have to do with growing up in New York?

CONNIE. It's just something I've observed.

SUZANNE. Well, it is a bubble in a sense. You think the rest of the world is the same way, racially diverse, tolerant, culturally alive –

CONNIE. There is an idealism in New York. A belief that anything is possible there…maybe we should move back.

SUZANNE. We always talk about moving back.

JONAS. Why don't you?

MATT. Too expensive. You can't live there.

JONAS. People live there, who aren't wealthy. In Brooklyn, or, I don't know…

MATT. Brooklyn's a fortune too.

SUZANNE. You have to live in Philadelphia now, if you want to live in New York.

MATT. And Suzanne needs a studio. It's just too much. We can't do it.

CONNIE. *(to* **SUZANNE***)* What do you think about how people are born? You never said.

SUZANNE. I think people are born good and stay good, but they don't always know it.

CONNIE. I like that. It's very poetic.

SUZANNE. Because when you feel the most like yourself, the most at peace, you are good in that moment, always.

JONAS. That's what I'm saying.

MATT. What about people who feel most themselves when they're perpetuating crimes against humanity. Terrorists. War criminals.

SUZANNE. I don't think they feel most like themselves at that time. I think they're dominated by their anger, their fear, at that time.

MATT. When do you think Hitler felt most like himself?

SUZANNE. When he was playing the violin, or the oboe, or – what did he play?

CONNIE. He played something?

SUZANNE. Wasn't he some kind of musician?

MATT. He was an artist. A painter.

SUZANNE. Really? I thought he was a musician. Are you sure?

CONNIE. Look it up.

JONAS. Connie feels no evening is complete until we've Googled up a new piece of information.

*(***SUZANNE*** goes to the computer.)*

SUZANNE. Matt thinks Wikipedia will save the planet.

JONAS. Really? I despise Wikipedia.

SUZANNE. You do?

JONAS. Uch. I don't want to feel like all my information has been fingered by sixteen year olds.

CONNIE. He's an information prude.

JONAS. I am. I'm for intellectual property. Despite my inability to claim any.

MATT. Exactly. It's absurd to try to own an idea. Ideas are like oxygen and the more we allow everyone to have equal access to information, the closer we'll be to a true democracy.

SUZANNE. And supposedly, after 2012 we'll all be psychic anyway. I mean, those of us who are still alive.

CONNIE. What is this thing about 2012?

JONAS. Just another end of the world date.

SUZANNE. The Mayans, according to the Mayan calendar. Some kind of apocalypse is coming.

CONNIE. In five years? Jesus. Maybe I'll ease up on the Botox, then.

SUZANNE. *(reading)* Hitler was a painter.

MATT. I think his failure as a painter was a big part of his whole deal, his whole evolution.

JONAS. If you believe the unpaid intern who wrote this entry.

SUZANNE. *(reading)* He was rejected from the Viennese Art Academy...

MATT. If only they'd let him in, the holocaust wouldn't have happened.

SUZANNE. Here! He tried to write an opera with a friend! He was a musician.

MATT. Nice try. *(at the computer)* Look, the guy was a painter. There are paintings from his youth. He was obsessed with art.

SUZANNE. The opera was about a leader trying to establish the Roman Empire by overthrowing the Papal government in Rome. "It was in that hour it all began." With the opera.

MATT. Maybe. But he was a painter.

CONNIE. How did we even get onto this?

MATT. The idea of goodness, when people are most themselves.

SUZANNE. Yes, well my point holds – he was happiest as a painter, got rejected and very bitter, as often happens, and you know turned all that creative energy into something destructive.

MATT. Yeah, but he can't have been a very good artist.

SUZANNE. So?

MATT. So maybe his highest calling was as an evil political leader. Maybe that's when he was at his most creative. I mean it took a lot of energy to wipe out the Jews and the gays.

SUZANNE. Mass murder can't be someone's highest calling.

MATT. It can if that's what they're best at. How do we know? We have such a limited perspective – maybe the species needed thinning at that time – like *biologically*, Germany was overpopulated.

SUZANNE. Are you defending the holocaust?

CONNIE. That's very controversial

MATT. I'm not defending it from a moral point of view, I'm just saying morality is limited. Nature isn't moral. If it were, there wouldn't be tornadoes and earthquakes in the poorest parts of the world, would there?

SUZANNE. I just don't think the holocaust was an act of Nature.

MATT. It was the act of a child of Nature, a human.

SUZANNE. Humans are not just children of Nature. They're children of God.

MATT. Uch.

SUZANNE. He doesn't like the word God.

CONNIE. It's an uncomfortable word. I totally agree.

SUZANNE. It doesn't have to be.

JONAS. It's been distorted.

SUZANNE. Yes. We have to reclaim it.

CONNIE. Who has the energy?

MATT. God is just a way to avoid taking responsibility for being good. There's always someone to forgive you, no matter how much of an asshole you are.

JONAS. That's one way to look at it. If you see God as outside of yourself.

CONNIE. Jonas has been very into Buddhism lately.

SUZANNE. Really, are you meditating?

JONAS. No, I'm just reading about meditating.

CONNIE. He's meditating on meditating.

SUZANNE. It's so hard. I try, but I can never stick with it for more than a week or two...

MATT. There's no God in Buddhism, is there?

JONAS. Well, in a sense there is, I think. The force of the universe. Or the highest truth.... But they don't use the word much, no. I think because of Christianity, actually.

MATT. Exactly. It's a stupid word. Let's just get rid of it.

JONAS. Well, Jews don't use the word.

CONNIE. But you know people hate Jews. We don't realize it, but they really do.

JONAS. Amber.

CONNIE. Exactly. *(to* SUZANNE*)* Big Brother.

MATT. Again.

JONAS. Yes!

CONNIE. She went on and on about how all Jews are just basically not nice. It was on You Tube.

JONAS. CBS was too cowardly to air it. Typical.

CONNIE. But where else could you see this unvarnished bigotry?

MATT. Any bar in the South.

CONNIE. I mean in pop culture –

JONAS. And who wants to go to a bar in the South?

SUZANNE. Talk about bigotry. All of you!

CONNIE. Honey, have you ever tried to find a salad in the South? Oh!

MATT. – I can say it. I'm from the South.

CONNIE. – I forgot to show you the baby!

JONAS. They don't need to see –

(CONNIE *pulls an ultra-sound picture out of her purse.*)

CONNIE. There he is! We just had the amnio.

SUZANNE. Wow.

(CONNIE *passes the picture to* MATT.)

CONNIE. Isn't it incredible? How you can see so much at 16 weeks? I mean, he's a person!

MATT. Yeah...

CONNIE. In this profile, he looks like Jonas, and in this one he looks like me.

SUZANNE. Yeah...

CONNIE. The doctor said he was unusually good looking.

JONAS. He says that to everyone. This doctor thinks no one will be satisfied unless they hear their kid is the best he ever saw.

CONNIE. Yes, but he really is quite stunning.

SUZANNE. You really can see his features.

CONNIE. It's why the anti-abortion people are doing so well now.

MATT. Yes, we all know that.

SUZANNE. He does really look like a person.

CONNIE. He's unusually well-defined, I think.

(SUZANNE *starts crying.*)

MATT. Let's, let's, it's time for dinner.

CONNIE. Suze...?

SUZANNE. Sorry. Sorry.

CONNIE. What is it?

SUZANNE. Nothing. I'm sorry.

MATT. Let's just – let's go in –

CONNIE. Suze. Tell me. Please.

SUZANNE. I had another miscarriage. Last week.

CONNIE. Oh my God. I didn't even know –

SUZANNE. We weren't very far along –

CONNIE. Why didn't you tell me?

SUZANNE. I don't know. I was going to –

CONNIE. Oh my God.

JONAS. I'm sorry Suzanne.

SUZANNE. I was only 9 weeks – but, I'm sorry.

MATT. Let's just – let's go inside.

CONNIE. I feel horrible.

SUZANNE. It's okay. How would you know? I'm sorry for making a big deal of it.

CONNIE. It is a big deal.

SUZANNE. I'm okay. I'm okay. Let's just…go inside.

(**MATT** and **SUZANNE** go inside.)

JONAS. You have to stop showing everyone those pictures.

(**CONNIE** sighs as they go inside, leaving the lights on the red painting.)

Scene Two

(**MATT** and **SUZANNE** *clean up dinner.*)

MATT. Those fuckers get every fucking thing. Everything just falls into their fucking laps.

SUZANNE. That's not true.

MATT. What don't they have?

SUZANNE. I don't know…a lot of things.

MATT. They're rich. He's a big fucking success and she's got all this stupid power. And they're rich.

SUZANNE. You said rich twice.

MATT. Well they are rich twice. They're rich many times. Doesn't she come from money?

SUZANNE. Sort of. Not really.

MATT. More than we do.

SUZANNE. I guess. I mean, we went to the same school…

MATT. You were on a scholarship.

SUZANNE. But we had the same opportunities.

MATT. But you had to work a lot of harder for it.

SUZANNE. She always worked hard.

MATT. She had connections to get her job.

SUZANNE. What's the point of this?

MATT. They didn't even try to get pregnant –

SUZANNE. They must've tried a little…

MATT. They got married a year ago and bang, they've got a kid, like she's twenty –

SUZANNE. She always wanted kids.

MATT. And they'll have ten nannies so they never even have to see the kid –

SUZANNE. You don't know that.

MATT. Yeah, like either one of them's going to stay home with a baby.

SUZANNE. He's killing his voice.

MATT. What do you mean?

SUZANNE. He's always been one of those people who just needs to succeed, you know? To survive. So he just takes everyone's notes, and I don't think he even realizes how sort of generic his writing is now –

MATT. He definitely does not.

SUZANNE. And you know, I read one of the novels he couldn't get published and it was this really beautiful weird little story. It was so much more…humane.

MATT. No one wants humanity.

SUZANNE. And she's a failed actress.

MATT. Well that explains a lot. *(pause)* Everyone here wishes they were something else.

SUZANNE. Not just here.

MATT. But here there's this feeling like they're owed. In Bangladesh no one feels they're owed.

SUZANNE. Well, they'll get it in the next life, I guess.

MATT. Right, the less we believe in an afterlife, the more we think we deserve it all now. Well, that's Marx, I guess.

SUZANNE. It always comes back to Marx.

MATT. Marx and Bob Dylan.

SUZANNE. I'm just saying they haven't gotten everything they ever wanted.

MATT. They still have a lot more than most people.

SUZANNE. So do you. Have a lot more than most people. In the world. Starting with where you were born.

MATT. Yeah, I know I'm supposed to be so grateful for my running water and my sneakers, but my childhood was fucking brutal –

SUZANNE. If it wasn't how it was, you wouldn't be how you are.

MATT. Exactly.

SUZANNE. I mean, you wouldn't be compassionate, or creative, or any of the good things you are, either.

MATT. I'm just saying things could have been a lot easier for me if my Dad wasn't a violent drunk and my Mom wasn't fucking insane.

SUZANNE. Easier, but maybe not better.

MATT. I'm just so sick of struggling. Nothing has ever come easy for me –

SUZANNE. Why should it? If we wanted to be rich, we'd go to business school. Do you want to go to business school? Go ahead.

MATT. First of all, I could never get into business school today. Do you know what's going on out there? Kids are being trained to get into business school in the womb. They're getting SAT tutors when they're embryos.

(SUZANNE sighs.)

MATT. What? I'm sorry, I just want you to acknowledge that life isn't fair.

SUZANNE. I never said it was fair…

MATT. Well you look like you're mad at me for thinking that sometimes people get screwed for no good reason.

SUZANNE. I'm not mad at you. It's just a little…depressing.

MATT. We can disagree.

SUZANNE. I know.

MATT. It doesn't mean I don't love you.

SUZANNE. I know.

MATT. It doesn't mean you don't love me. Does it?

SUZANNE. No. It's just depressing. To live with. A little.

MATT. Well sometimes it can be hard to live with your attitude too.

SUZANNE. But isn't my attitude a lot more, sort of, positive?

MATT. It's positive but it's like, there's no room for being pissed off about anything. Everything always has to be okay, even when it really isn't.

SUZANNE. But that's all I have.

(She gets increasingly sad.)

MATT. I'm sorry. But being pissed off is all I have.

(She starts to cry.)

SUZANNE. It's just, hard to maintain…by myself.

MATT. You don't have to maintain it then. Get upset. It sucks to lose three babies. It sucks. It sucks that we can't afford the IVF and the insurance companies pay for my father's Viagra so he can fuck women half his age and our fucking premiums cover everyone else's ultrasounds so they can shove them in your face all day –

SUZANNE. We could afford IVF...

MATT. If the fucking health insurance industry wasn't so fucked in this country –

SUZANNE. If we got different kinds of jobs...

MATT. You just said that's not what we're about.

SUZANNE. I said it's not what we've chosen to focus on.

MATT. You're making a living. How many artists can say that? And now you want to stop doing the only thing that's working in your life so you can keep trying to do the thing that doesn't work?

SUZANNE. I want a baby.

MATT. So the fuck do I. But, unlike Connie and Jonas, we don't get every fucking thing handed to us on a silver platter. We have to struggle and fail and deal with death and mice and the holes in the fucking roof and our cocksucking mortality –

SUZANNE. Matt. Shh. Stop. Stop. STOP.

(Silence. She wipes her eyes with her sleeve. He gets her a Kleenex.)

MATT. I'm sorry.

SUZANNE. I can't take it.

MATT. I'm sorry.

SUZANNE. I can't take it.

MATT. Can't take what? Me?

SUZANNE. I don't know.

MATT. What do you mean?

SUZANNE. Maybe. *(pause)* I mean, just, right now.

MATT. Because of the hormones, right?

SUZANNE. I just...I can't live in your world right now. This world of random punishments and persecutions.

MATT. Well what do you want me to do? I don't see things the way you do –

SUZANNE. The way you see things is death. It's murder.

MATT. Murder?

SUZANNE. I feel like it's killing me, and you, and everything around us.

(long pause)

MATT. We just have to ride this out. The hormones.

SUZANNE. It's not the hormones.

MATT. Honey, trust me. The hormones are a major factor here.

SUZANNE. What hormones do you have to blame?

MATT. Yours.

SUZANNE. Yeah.

MATT. Not that I blame them.

SUZANNE. You blame everything. Your parents. Connie. Hollywood. The environment, the power lines, there's always a reason your life is...blighted, and the reason is never you. Hormones. You fuck.

MATT. I forgot the most basic rule of being a man.

SUZANNE. What?

MATT. Never mention hormones.

SUZANNE. If that's the most basic rule of being a man, then being a man must be pretty fucking trivial. I don't know how a man like that gets through a single day. With that as his guiding fucking principle.

MATT. It was a joke.

SUZANNE. I wish it were funny.

MATT. It would be funny if you weren't pulsating with hormones at the moment.

SUZANNE. You can't even honor your own pathetic little basic rule.

MATT. It's not my basic rule.

SUZANNE. What is your basic rule? "Always be an asshole?"

MATT. The sarcasm isn't helping your argument, by the way.

SUZANNE. What is your basic rule, then?

MATT. I don't have a basic rule, Suzanne. Only assholes have a basic rule. Do you have a basic rule?

SUZANNE. Yes, actually.

MATT. What is it?

SUZANNE. "Grow. Grow or die now."

MATT. Well you can't argue with that.

SUZANNE. But you do.

MATT. I'm not.

SUZANNE. But you won't grow. You just want to die. You just want to be angry and kill everything.

MATT. You've got to stop saying that.

SUZANNE. I'm sorry.

MATT. And I am growing.

SUZANNE. How? In what way?

MATT. I'm married.

SUZANNE. Yes, that was growth. It was six years ago.

MATT. Settling down, getting a real job. I've grown a lot.

SUZANNE. Okay, but it doesn't mean you get to stop now. When it's hard.

MATT. I haven't stopped growing. I just ran out of money.

(**SUZANNE** *starts crying.*)

SUZANNE. I can't just give up.

MATT. I'm not saying we have to give up. I don't think we even need the stupid IVF.

SUZANNE. It's not just the IVF. It's the PGD.

MATT. Whatever. We just have to keep trying. We get pregnant.

SUZANNE. He said we could keep having miscarriages, if we don't get the PGD.

MATT. Maybe, he said. There's no reason –

SUZANNE. – No reason he could tell. He's not a specialist.

MATT. Look, someone has to have the bad luck. If the miscarriage rates are, whatever, thirty percent and some women never miscarry, then some have to miscarry, you know, a lot.

SUZANNE. But what if we keep getting tails? Every time we flip the coin. And he said our odds are worse now. After three miscarriages.

MATT. I just think he's wrong. *(pause)* And you don't want to take all those drugs….

SUZANNE. Of course, but I just don't think I can go through it again.

MATT. Yeah.

SUZANNE. The heartbeat.

MATT. I know.

(pause)

SUZANNE. I didn't even want kids. I was fine. I was happy.

MATT. I know. I'm sorry.

SUZANNE. After the first time, I was relieved, almost.

MATT. You weren't ready.

SUZANNE. It was the second one –

MATT. Yeah.

SUZANNE. I spent the whole time convincing myself I could do it.

MATT. I know.

SUZANNE. I talked to every artist I know who has kids and every single one said it was the best thing that ever happened to them. After that, you can't go back.

(pause)

MATT. I don't know what to do, Suze. I just don't know how we afford it. Tell me.

SUZANNE. I just think, we're educated, we're you know, competent. We have…skills.

MATT. We barely have health insurance.

SUZANNE. Well, it's crazy. We have to stop living like we're twenty-five.

MATT. When we were twenty-five, we didn't have health insurance at all. I mean, we finally got things to be sort of on an even keel – like we almost know we can make the rent every month, and now you want to compromise even more?

SUZANNE. Maybe you should…try…to make money with your music.

MATT. I have tried. I did try.

SUZANNE. I mean, like give Connie and Jonas your demo. For example.

MATT. They've heard me play. If they were dying to buy one of my songs, I think they would.

SUZANNE. Sometimes you have to ask for things. In life.

MATT. You mean, as a favor?

SUZANNE. Or advice even. If they have any ideas for work –

MATT. What ideas are they going to have that I haven't had?

SUZANNE. I don't know, like maybe there's a character in some show who's a musician and they need someone to write the music, or play the music even…

(MATT *just stares at her.*)

SUZANNE. Please don't look at me like I'm an idiot.

MATT. I just think you're living in a fantasy world. I tried, for years, to make it as a musician, and it sucked and I sucked –

SUZANNE. You didn't suck –

MATT. As a person, I sucked.

SUZANNE. Oh.

MATT. And you know, I made a choice, to have a family –

SUZANNE. But why does it have to be music or family?

MATT. Because you can't be successful in music and care about anyone else besides yourself.

SUZANNE. Of course you can. What about Bono? Sting? They give back…

MATT. I'm telling you. To get to the point where you have money to give back, you have to be totally focused on yourself for so long that you forget how to be a real person. Trust me. Even Bob Dylan. Total asshole at home.

SUZANNE. This is insane.

MATT. It's not. It's reality. Like Jonas – you can be successful or real –

SUZANNE. So you're saying I'm not successful? Or not real?

MATT. You're a little successful, but not that much. Really successful people – they're not nice. Even Gandhi. Asshole to his wife. Einstein. JFK. Martin Luther King. It's not just rock music. It's everything. Even Jesus was an asshole. He couldn't commit to Mary Magdalene. He couldn't have kids. He had an agenda.

SUZANNE. A mission. A mission of love, for fuck's sake.

MATT. He wanted to be immortal. He wanted people to know his name.

SUZANNE. That's a really insane thing to say about Jesus.

MATT. He was human. Isn't that the whole point?

SUZANNE. The best possible human.

MATT. But human nonetheless.

(SUZANNE *sighs.*)

SUZANNE. I'm not saying you should try to be as successful as Jesus. Or Sting. I'm just saying you could try to make a little more money.

MATT. There's no middle ground in music. You're a star or you're shit.

SUZANNE. Oh my God!

MATT. It's not pretty. But it's true.

SUZANNE. You think you gave up trying to be successful so you could be a nice guy. But you know, you're not that nice a guy.

MATT. Thanks.

SUZANNE. I mean, you say you did it for me? I didn't ask for that. I'm asking for this. Okay? I'm asking for this.

(*MATT sighs and collapses on a chair.* SUZANNE *comes to him and strokes his hair. He buries his face in her belly. The lights fade.*)

(*In the darkness, a woman's voice murmurs.*)

VOICE OF ACTRESS. Sorry, I must have taken a wrong turn.

Scene Three

(Lights come up on **CONNIE** *and* **JONAS** *in their big living room, watching dailies we don't see.)*

ACTRESS. Sorry, I must have taken a wrong turn.

DIRECTOR. Again.

CONNIE. She gets better.

ACTRESS. Oh no! I think I went the wrong way!

JONAS. God.

CONNIE. I know. But Gary worked with her, and she really gets better in the later takes.

JONAS. All I can see are her lips.

CONNIE. Yeah –

JONAS. They're a different size in every scene.

CONNIE. I know, she's got a problem with collagen.

JONAS. How's anyone going to be able to watch the movie?

CONNIE. It's in her contract exactly how big we want them and she keeps sneaking out to get more on her off days.

JONAS. She's deranged.

CONNIE. She's America's sweetheart. What are you going to do? Here. These are from the end of the day –

(She fumbles through a pile of DVDS.)

God, being on the set is so much more fun now that everyone knows I'm pregnant.

JONAS. Because you can puke freely without people thinking you're bulimic?

CONNIE. No – although that is a relief. It's just I never realized how much it equalizes everyone. I had grips coming up to me to tell me about their wives pregnancies, and hair and make-up – they're all pulling out their baby pictures. I just really felt like one of the people.

JONAS. The world loves a mother.

CONNIE. They love a pregnant woman, that's for sure. The PAs were all worried about getting me a nice chair, and not because I can fire them, at all. For the first time they saw me as...I don't know...

JONAS. Vulnerable?

CONNIE. Ich. Maybe. It's gross really, isn't it?

JONAS. Gross and beautiful.

CONNIE. It was beautiful. The warmth. For the first time, I really had something to talk about with the crew. I felt like I could sit with any of them at lunch...

JONAS. Did you?

CONNIE. No. But I could have.

JONAS. That's nice. Maybe next time you should.

CONNIE. And there's something so.... comforting about this feeling that there's always someone with me. Now that he's more of a person.... I'm never alone.

JONAS. Mm.... And it's the only time you'll ever have a penis and a vagina.

CONNIE. And two hearts. *(pause)* Did you give Matt's demo to Nolan?

JONAS. Yes.

CONNIE. Well, did he listen to it?

JONAS. Probably not.

CONNIE. Did you tell him he's a friend?

JONAS. He's not a friend. Of mine, really.

CONNIE. He's friend enough. I think you should follow up.

JONAS. You know, I'm not, personally, interested in Matt's music.

CONNIE. Well, you may not be, but a lot of people are.

JONAS. Not that many. Obviously. Not enough.

CONNIE. That's not fair. As you know. *(pause)* I just feel bad for them.

JONAS. I feel bad for them.

CONNIE. There's just so much struggle.

JONAS. I'd rather send them to a good fertility doctor than a music supervisor.

CONNIE. Well, they can't afford that, at this point.

JONAS. Right, I just don't think this is the solution.

CONNIE. Well it could be. I mean, he's just as good as half the people Nolan uses.

JONAS. The people Nolan uses are professionals.

CONNIE. God, you're really a snob. Matt's a professional. He was, anyway. He had a huge following in Portland.

JONAS. In Portland. Ten years ago.

CONNIE. Portland has a major music scene.

JONAS. You know, I'm not a believer that everyone has a right to a career as an artist. If you don't have the drive, or the talent, or whatever –

CONNIE. There are so many brilliant artists who were failures in their time.

JONAS. Not that many.

CONNIE. Van Gogh.

JONAS. Who else?

CONNIE. A million. Everyone always says.

JONAS. Okay, but who?

CONNIE. Let's look it up.

(She goes to the computer, Googles.)

CONNIE. Renoir. "As with many other artists, Renoir was not famous until after his death."

JONAS. Who are the other ones?

CONNIE. I don't know. I can't find a list…

JONAS. I think it's a myth. Basically, you have your lifetime. And success may not be a measure of worth, but it is a measure of relevance to your time. So, it doesn't matter how brilliant you are if you can't connect to your audience. And maybe the work you do that's best, is the work that you think is the most inane, or lowest common denominator, but it's good because it means something to the most people.

CONNIE. Are you talking to yourself?

JONAS. Maybe. I guess I'm saying that the masses, the market, has a wisdom of its own. The yearning of one's time.

CONNIE. That's so simplistic. What about marketing? The critics? The fact that most of the audience are idiots who don't want to be challenged in any way?

JONAS. Then that's the time. If people need to be soothed, then the soothers will be successful. It's the soothers who are needed. Not the challengers. The challengers are the idiots.

CONNIE. Fine. I just want you to ask Nolan to listen to Matt's demo.

JONAS. Okay. *(She looks at him.)* Now?

CONNIE. Just send him an email so we can move on with our lives.

(She hands him his Blackberry. He types as she cues up another DVD.)

JONAS. You don't even like Matt.

CONNIE. I want to help them. Their poverty makes me uncomfortable.

JONAS. You mean you feel guilty for showing them the sonogram.

CONNIE. Why did I do that?

JONAS. You're excited.

CONNIE. I just wasn't thinking, at all.

JONAS. Well, next time, you'll think.

CONNIE. It was the Kennel Hora.

JONAS. Kenahora. And it's not a noun.

CONNIE. What is it, again?

JONAS. Just, you don't...flaunt things –

CONNIE. – or you get punished.

JONAS. No –

CONNIE. You get the evil eye!

JONAS. Some people see it that way. Like you'll get cursed. But I think it's just about kindness – toward people who may not have as much as you do.

CONNIE. Right. Right. It's a little codependent, but it's nice.

JONAS. It's not codependent. It's sensitive. Giving Nolan Matt's demo is codependent.

CONNIE. Oh, I think this is her good take. *(She reaches for the remote, then her cell phone rings, so she picks that up too.)* Oh good, it's Costigan, finally.

JONAS. Ask him why it took so long –

CONNIE. Hello? Hi. Right…So, what does that mean? But –

JONAS. What?

CONNIE. What do we do? How long does that take? But what are the chances – ? I know, but statistically – Well, yes, we'll come right now…Okay.

(She puts down the phone.)

JONAS. What?

CONNIE. There's something wrong.

JONAS. What is it?

CONNIE. Something with the baby's chromosomes.

JONAS. Is it Downs?

CONNIE. No. It's something, I couldn't even absorb it – we have to give blood…if one of us carries this thing, then maybe it'll be okay…I don't know…I don't know.

(She starts crying.)

JONAS. I'm sure I carry it. Some weird chromosome? Look at my family!

CONNIE. Really?

JONAS. It's going to be fine.

CONNIE. We have to go give blood. We have to go now.

(They fumble for their jackets and keys.)

Scene Four

*(Sitting in her studio, **SUZANNE** watches "The Secret"
on her computer. **MATT** enters and watches with her.
From the computer come the Voice of a Man speaking
with intensity.)*

MAN. Everything that's around you now, in your life,
including the things you're complaining about, you've
attracted. Now I know at first blush, that's going to be
something you hate to hear. You're immediately going
to say "I didn't attract that car accident, I didn't attract
this particular client, I didn't particularly attract this
debt…Whatever it happens to be that you're complaining about and I'm here to be a little bit in your
face and to say, yes you did attract it.

MATT. What the fuck is this?

SUZANNE. It's better than it looks.

MAN. And this is one of the hardest concepts to get but
once you've accepted it, it's life transforming. This is
part of the overall giant secret here.

*(**MATT** picks up the box.)*

MATT. "The Secret."

(Another Man's Voice comes from the computer.)

MAN #2. And most of us attract by default, we just think we
have no control over any of it. Our thoughts are on
auto-pilot. Our feelings are on auto pilot and so everything is just brought to us by default.

MATT. "This is the secret to everything –

*(**SUZANNE** turns down the volume.)*

MATT. – joy, health, money, relationships, love, happiness…
everything you have ever wanted!"

SUZANNE. You don't have to watch it. Go outside and spit
tobacco on the lawn.

(She pauses the DVD.)

MATT. How much did you spend on this?

SUZANNE. Not that much!

MATT. Thirty-five dollars!?

SUZANNE. I got it on sale. And it's very inspiring.

MATT. Well, sure, who wouldn't want the secret to everything?

SUZANNE. It's so easy to be a skeptic. I mean I know faith is really really un...hip. But the people who believe in something are the ones who make things happen. In fact, we make everything we believe in happen. That's what they're saying – the bad things too.

MATT. "Worrying is just praying for what you don't want."

SUZANNE. Exactly. What's that from?

MATT. It sounds like AA. It's crazy how those stupid slogans stick in your head. Years later.

SUZANNE. Because they're not stupid. They just sound stupid.

MATT. They're pretty stupid.

SUZANNE. Well you're not exactly in a position to judge.

MATT. Why not?

SUZANNE. You quit. You quit AA.

MATT. That puts me in a perfect position to judge. I tried it and decided it was stupid.

SUZANNE. You never surrendered.

MATT. I don't see you going to Al-anon.

SUZANNE. I know, but I should. I know I should.

MATT. Because you think I'm an alcoholic?

SUZANNE. Because I'm totally codependant. I know I am.

MATT. Then go. What's stopping you?

SUZANNE. I don't know.... It was so much easier to go together. It was like a fun thing we did on Thursday night.

MATT. Yeah, I didn't think it was so fun.

(**SUZANNE** *sighs.*)

SUZANNE. I really enjoyed it. I liked having...a system. A shared belief system. A spiritual vocabulary.

MATT. For idiots. Like all religion. So you don't have to think for yourself.

SUZANNE. That's so, not – AA is very open to interpretation. Or, whatever. Self-definition. "Higher power!" It can be anything. It can be your dog.

MATT. Blech.

SUZANNE. I've got to raise my frequency.

(She turns "The Secret" back on.)

MATT. Why did they do all these weird little re-enactments? They hired actors, and went out with a film crew for this?

SUZANNE. It's not great cinema, but you can't argue with the Law of Attraction.

MATT. Yes you can. I can.

SUZANNE. You can't because you're a living example. I mean, we all are.

MATT. How am I a living example?

SUZANNE. You have what you believe you can have. And nothing more.

MATT. So you believe you can't have a baby?

SUZANNE. Maybe, on some level, I do. Or did. Maybe I think, I thought, I don't deserve it, or I can't handle it.

MATT. So you created your own miscarriages.

SUZANNE. Well, not literally…

MATT. And the teenage welfare mother –

SUZANNE. Believes she can have babies, but doesn't believe she can go to college, or whatever.

MATT. And your mother's cancer?

SUZANNE. Well, I don't want to be incendiary –

MATT. But what?

SUZANNE. She had a lot of self-hatred. She did.

MATT. And the children who are born with, whatever, Cystic Fibrosis?

SUZANNE. I don't know about them.

MATT. I'm sure their parents would want to ram this DVD down your throat.

SUZANNE. That's aggressive. *(She tries to make sense of it.)* Maybe…the illness of the child is a manifestation of the rage of the parent?

MATT. That's beyond deranged.

(He goes to the kitchen. **SUZANNE** *turns "The Secret" back on.* **MATT** *comes out with a beer.* **SUZANNE** *looks at it.)*

MATT. Want one?

SUZANNE. I really think you should watch this with me.

MATT. You bought this for me, to be my little pep talk?

SUZANNE. No, I needed to raise my frequency. My life is a mirror of my beliefs. I don't want to just sit around complaining about how everyone else has everything I want and life isn't fair.

MATT. I gave Jonas my demo. The guy never called me.

SUZANNE. I gave Jonas your demo.

MATT. So, what?

SUZANNE. So, it's not something someone else can do for you.

MATT. I never asked you to! I thought this whole thing was about you taking responsibility.

SUZANNE. It is, but I feel like I need you to be…involved. I can't do it alone!

MATT. Do what?

SUZANNE. Manifest a baby!

MATT. Manifest a baby?

SUZANNE. It's cheaper than getting IVF. If we imagine our child. If we believe that our child is here. We could make the nursery…

MATT. That seems very sick. And very depressing. An empty nursery?

SUZANNE. We can't see it that way. We have to see it as making room in our hearts, by making room in our house. Inviting the universe to put a baby in the crib.

MATT. What do we say to people when they come over and see the empty nursery?

SUZANNE. That's the wrong attitude. No one has to know about the nursery. It'll be *our* nursery. We can use it as, like…a temple until the baby comes. We can meditate in there, or make love even, it can be the place where love happens in this house.

MATT. So where's the spiritual nursery going to be?

SUZANNE. Over there…?

MATT. We give up our dining area so we can have a secret love…zone for a child who doesn't exist?

SUZANNE. Love is food for the soul! Food is just food for the body.

MATT. *(softening)* You've really lost your mind.

SUZANNE. Isn't it nice though? Just the idea of love being more important than food? Isn't it just so true?

MATT. Food is really boring.

SUZANNE. Food *is* really boring!

MATT. And we're all supposed to act like it's so interesting! I'm tired of pretending that prawns have meaning.

SUZANNE. See? Isn't it a relief?

(**SUZANNE** *starts clearing books and objects off of shelves.*)

MATT. What are you doing?

SUZANNE. We have to get rid of everything that's cluttering up our spiritual space.

MATT. I'm not throwing out my Noam Chomsky. *(grabbing a book)* De Tocqueville?!

SUZANNE. Just find a new place for it.

(**SUZANNE** *clears with increasing intensity.*)

MATT. My Hendrix pick?

SUZANNE. Oh, we can leave that. But just things we really want to manifest.

(**MATT** *starts sorting through his objects.*)

SUZANNE. I can already feel the frequency rising!

(**SUZANNE** *keeps clearing.*)

Scene Five

(CONNIE lies on an exam table. JONAS holds her hand.
DR. COSTIGAN enters.)

DR. COSTIGAN. So, we just got the second set of tests back.

CONNIE. And?

DR. COSTIGAN. It's not good.

(He starts to put the wand on CONNIE's belly.)

JONAS. Not good what?

DR. COSTIGAN. There's a chromosomal imbalance, result-
ing in an excess of genetic information.

CONNIE. So, so –

DR. COSTIGAN. He's not going to make it.

CONNIE. Oh my God.

DR. COSTIGAN. *(looking at the ultrasound)* Yeah. You can see
it now.

JONAS. What?

DR. COSTIGAN. He's struggling. Even if he makes it all the
way through the pregnancy, which is unlikely, he won't
live long. Do you want to see?

CONNIE. *(looking away)* No!

DR. COSTIGAN. This should make it easier. The decision.
You don't really have a decision.

CONNIE. But just a month ago, you said he was perfect –

DR. COSTIGAN. A lot can change. In a month. The heart
has stopped developing. The brain too, it looks like.

CONNIE. But how –

DR. COSTIGAN. In a case like this, we recommend an imme-
diate termination.

(A sound escapes CONNIE.)

JONAS. Termination?

DR. COSTIGAN. We'll get you into the clinic that does these.
They're very good.

JONAS. Wait, wait, wait –

CONNIE. – but isn't there anything else we can – ?

DR. COSTIGAN. We have to do this fast. *(calling)* Karen? Can we get them in tomorrow? *(to CONNIE)* Don't worry. We can get you in, in time.

CONNIE. In time?

DR. COSTIGAN. Legally. We're right at the cut off here.

CONNIE. Oh my God.

> (CONNIE *sobs.* JONAS *holds her arm.*)

DR. COSTIGAN. I'm going to prescribe some anti-anxiety medication.

CONNIE. Oh my God.

JONAS. It's okay. We're going to be okay.

CONNIE. No.

DR. COSTIGAN. Did you talk to one of the genetic counselors?

JONAS. Yes.

DR. COSTIGAN. So you've been over all of that?

JONAS. All of what?

DR. COSTIGAN. Did he say if either of you carry this?

JONAS. We don't.

DR. COSTIGAN. So it's just a fluke, then. You can try again, soon enough.

CONNIE. Try again?

DR. COSTIGAN. In just a few months, okay? Don't worry, we'll get this handled right away for you.

> (He exits. An **ANESTHESIOLOGIST** enters and wheels **CONNIE** into a circle of light as **JONAS** stands in a separate waiting area, staring at a fish tank.)

> (The **ANESTHESIOLOGIST** puts a mask over **CONNIE**'s face.)

ANESTHESIOLOGIST. Count backwards from ten.

CONNIE. Ten, nine...eigh...t., sev...en...si...x...fi....

> (The **ANESTHESIOLOGIST** exits.)

(The lights rise dimly on **MATT** *as he plays guitar and sings James Taylor's "Lo & Behold.")*

MATT. "Lonely by day, empty and cold.
Only to say. Lo and Behold.
Deep in the night. Down in my dreams.
Glorious sight, this soul has seen."

(In the now empty dining area, **SUZANNE** *pins up images of babies and mothers on the wall.)*

MATT. "There's a well on the hill. You just can't kill for Jesus. There's a well on the hill. Let it be.

*(***CONNIE*** *lies unconscious.)*

"Everybody's talking about the gospel story.
Some shall sink and some shall rise.
Everyone's talking 'bout the train to glory.
Long long time til it gets here to you baby."

*(***JONAS*** *is alone with the fish.)*

End of Act One

ACT TWO

MORE THAN A YEAR LATER.

Scene One

(CONNIE and SUZANNE sit by the pool outside Connie's beautiful house in the hills. SUZANNE is four months pregnant.)

SUZANNE. All I can eat is pasta Bolognese. All day long. And bread. Well, you know, you were nauseous, weren't you?

CONNIE. Horribly.

SUZANNE. I just can't believe I'm already so fat. Did you dye your hair at all?

CONNIE. I did.

SUZANNE. I thought so.

CONNIE. The semi-permanent kind. The kind that fades.

SUZANNE. It's so hard to know which of these things are real. Like herbal teas – in that book –

CONNIE. "What to Expect?"

SUZANNE. Right. No herbal teas, they say –

CONNIE. I know.

SUZANNE. I mean, chamomile? It seems extreme. And all the food groups – did you manage to eat all those vitamin A foods every single day?

CONNIE. Could we not talk about my pregnancy? I don't know why you'd want to use it as a reference anyway. It didn't go well.

SUZANNE. I'm sorry. I'm really sorry. *(pause)* I just didn't know – should I talk about it with you – would you want things to just be normal, or...?

CONNIE. Why would I want to talk about what you should eat? *You* want to talk about it – and I understand, being pregnant is like being brainwashed. It's all you can think about.

SUZANNE. You're possessed by an alien life form!

(pause)

CONNIE. Yeah.

(pause)

SUZANNE. I can't even really paint anymore – the fumes are so toxic, they make me feel sick and God only know what they're doing to the baby!

*(**CONNIE** glares at **SUZANNE**.)*

SUZANNE. Sorry. I'm just not sure how to be...real. I mean, do you want me to not talk about what's going on for me?

CONNIE. Yes.

SUZANNE. You want me to censor myself?

CONNIE. Yes. *(pause)* Talk about other things. Is that so hard? If you had a friend who was a paraplegic, would you feel compelled to talk about how much fun you had skiing?

(pause)

SUZANNE. So, how's work?

CONNIE. It sucks.

SUZANNE. It does? Why?

CONNIE. Because, truly, who cares?

SUZANNE. You used to care.

CONNIE. Yeah, well. Now I don't.

(pause)

SUZANNE. Have you guys...tried again?

CONNIE. What do think I've been doing, this whole time?

SUZANNE. I don't know. You haven't really talked to me about it.

CONNIE. Because all you ever do is ask me if I'm going to try again.

SUZANNE. Is that bad?

CONNIE. Everyone does it. It makes them feel better about what happened. Even the OB, while he's writing out the number of the abortionist, he's talking about trying again. Like the fact that we can try again will somehow erase what's happening. A death. A murder, really. A mercy killing, I guess. Mercy. What does it mean, really, Mercy.

(She gets out her iPhone and looks it up.)

I don't know why, looking things up online is the only thing I still really enjoy. At least, I can still get information. *(reading)* "Mercy. Compassion or forgiveness shown toward someone whom it is within one's power to punish or harm: the boy was screaming and begging for mercy. The mercies of God." You know the abortionist, she was this totally evil woman. Like ice. She looked at the ultrasound and she asked me, suspiciously, really, what was wrong with the baby. Like maybe there was some kind of mistake. And he was fine. Totally fine. According to what she could see. Three days before, the specialist told me he was dying. Dying before he was born. How did it feel? To be growing and deteriorating at the same time? Trying to move toward life while Death pulls you back. My little boy.

CONNIE. *(reading again)* "Mercy. An event to be grateful for, especially because its occurrence prevents something unpleasant or provides relief from suffering: his death was a mercy." So, yes, it provided relief from suffering, for him, apparently. But for us, it just made us a suffer a different way.

(Pause. **SUZANNE** *strokes her belly.)*

SUZANNE. Have you seen "The Secret?"

CONNIE. What secret?

SUZANNE. This video – it's a book too – about self-actualization –

CONNIE. That crap on Oprah?

SUZANNE. Do you watch Oprah?

CONNIE. Jonas does. He watches every piece of shit under the sun. He's in love with Oprah. I think she's a crazy bitch.

SUZANNE. Well, she's obviously a deeply inspiring person.

CONNIE. She needs therapy. She needs to work out her childhood shit.

SUZANNE. So, did you see the one about "The Secret?"

CONNIE. I heard about it. It sounded totally inane.

SUZANNE. Maybe, but it's not. It's based on this metaphysical principle – The Law of Attraction – that your thoughts create your feelings and your feelings create your reality. You manifest what you believe. Like if you think negative thoughts like "I'm so fat" then you will be fat.

CONNIE. Because you are fat, probably.

SUZANNE. Yes, but you always will be if you think of yourself that way. It's based on a universal principle.

CONNIE. The Law of Attraction.

SUZANNE. Like the Law of Gravity. Or the Law of Relativity.

CONNIE. But it's not scientific.

SUZANNE. It is. I think. That's what they're saying.

CONNIE. Let's look it up.

(She picks up her iPhone.)

SUZANNE. Anyway, these people, I mean, it's all very Power of Positive Thinking, which you can't argue with –

CONNIE. You can if you're feeling negative.

SUZANNE. Yes, but you'd just be proving them right. They say if you believe you already have what you want, and take steps to get it, then you generate this energy of abundance, or whatever, and it just comes to you.

CONNIE. And this is how you got pregnant.

SUZANNE. Yes. I really think so. I mean it took a while, but I visualized a baby and really focused on the feeling of having a child and *(She snaps.)* it happened. We got a baby.

CONNIE. You don't have the baby yet.

SUZANNE. Well, practically.

CONNIE. Talk to me after the amnio.

SUZANNE. I'm not getting an amnio.

CONNIE. You're not getting an amnio.

SUZANNE. No. The chance of miscarriage –

CONNIE. – is lower than the risk of Downs. At our age.

SUZANNE. I know, but I wouldn't be able to do anything about it, anyway....

(CONNIE *glares at* SUZANNE. *Then reads from her phone screen.*)

CONNIE. "Law of Attraction." Goes back to Hinduism.... it's a concept. An idea. Not a scientific principle. It's not a "Law."

(SUZANNE *reads off the screen.*)

SUZANNE. "The Buddha states 'what you become is the result of what you have thought.'"

CONNIE. The Buddha.

SUZANNE. Right.

CONNIE. He's not Einstein.

SUZANNE. He's the Buddha!

CONNIE. I'm just saying it's not provable.

SUZANNE. So what? God isn't provable either.

CONNIE. Exactly. God is bullshit.

SUZANNE. You can't say God is bullshit.

CONNIE. Why not? Are you the FCC?

SUZANNE. I just – something that almost every human being in history has believed in, in some form, can't be bullshit.

CONNIE. Well, God seems pretty limited, for an omnipotent deity – "He" can't even express himself in a way people can understand. I mean, network TV does a better job of communicating than God does, then. It's more of a unifier. God divides. American Idol brings the world together. That's why more people vote for American Idol than the president in this country. They just want to see some results.

SUZANNE. Are you mad at me?

CONNIE. No! Why? Do I seem angry?

SUZANNE. Well, yeah. Kind of.

CONNIE. Well, I am angry. I'm depressed and I'm sad. I feel a great deal of despair. But I'm fine. I'm functioning.

SUZANNE. Functioning isn't...you know....

CONNIE. It's a lot, Sweetie. It's a lot.

SUZANNE. Despair?

CONNIE. I feel...hope is impossible. I have no hope. No more.

SUZANNE. But why? There is hope. There's always *hope.*

CONNIE. I know there could be hope. One could have hope. Hope may even objectively exist. But I don't have it. I can't. It'll kill me. I've been screwed by Hope too many times. And right now, that's all I can see. Hope the deluder. Hope the humiliater. Hope that change is possible. That this country, for example, will ever be anything but an empty brain between two ears. That's how it looks to me. New York and California are like these two organs that hear the truth and between them is this big leering face on top of a greedy tub of lard.

SUZANNE. It's about the country?

CONNIE. Yes. All the dead children. All those poor beautiful mothers whose sons have been slaughtered for nothing. And they brought it on themselves! They voted for it. Or they didn't vote. I tried to save their sons. I tried!

(She starts to cry.)

SUZANNE. Is it...? What is it?

CONNIE. This cocksucking IVF. The embryos are going backward now. They put five of these fuckers in me, and I swear to god, they went the wrong way! They were like running from my uterus. It's like no one wants to be my child. Even my own eggs can't stand me anymore. That's what I've become. An embryo scarer.

SUZANNE. I didn't even know you –

CONNIE. Uch. The GIFT and the ZIFT. ICSI, DICKSEY, and fucking Cottontail, I've done it all. And it's like every new technology we try makes me less pregnant than the last one.

SUZANNE. God, Connie. Why didn't you tell me?

CONNIE. You don't want to hear about it.

SUZANNE. I do!

CONNIE. You don't. Trust me. At first you'll feel bad for me, but then, in about ten minutes, I'll be ranting, because I've totally lost my mind, and you'll start thinking maybe I'm a little self-indulgent, what with all the real problems in the world, the war and the famine, I can't expect to have everything, and actually now that you think of it, I have gotten everything I ever wanted (which isn't true, at all, but I know you'll think it), so isn't it only fair that this one thing should evade me? Isn't there really a wonderful spiritual lesson, a character building exercise to be found in all this? And the less compassion I feel from you, the more shrill and intolerable I'll become until you'll move past thoughts like "Why doesn't she just adopt?" to "Maybe it's better she not be a mother actually. Some women really shouldn't, and Connie's always been a bit brittle, ambitious. She's not nurturing at all. Thank God she can't conceive. In fact, her infertility is yet another proof that God does in fact exist and is always making the best decisions for the greater good."

SUZANNE. Wow. You think I feel that way about you?

CONNIE. Everyone does.

SUZANNE. I don't think you're brittle. I love you.

(CONNIE *wells up.*)

CONNIE. Thanks. But I know I'm brittle. I don't expect you to be an idiot.

SUZANNE. I don't even know what brittle means, really.

CONNIE. It's what I am. At this point. I'm so brittle I'll break if you touch me.

(SUZANNE *reaches to hug* CONNIE. CONNIE *flinches.*)

CONNIE. Don't. Really. I can't take it.

(SUZANNE *steps back.*)

SUZANNE. I'm sorry.

CONNIE. Thanks.

(pause)

SUZANNE. Well, what about adoption?

CONNIE. It's not that I have anything against it, really. But when you go to these specialists, it's like, they're crack dealers, really. They're getting you hooked on their… product. Which is Hope actually. It's not like they say "I'm sorry, but you can't have a child." Infertility doesn't actually mean, Un-fertile. It means, not-so-fertile, not-the-fertilest. But it's not like they even tell you your chances are horribly bad. They say something like, you've got a 30 percent chance to conceive on each cycle, so you know, do the math, 4 cycles should do it. Then after you try the 4 cycles, it's on to the next technology. There are endless "protocols" they can try on you, if you've got the money. And if you do have the money, you go from thinking "thank God I have the money. I'm going to keep going with this until it pays off" to wishing you never could have afforded the first round. And you start out thinking you'd never shoot your body full of drugs that no one really knows what kind of cancer they might cause for you, or your child. And then five years later, you've injected so many synthetic hormones, it's a miracle you haven't grown a second vagina. You know you can Just Adopt. But you're not going to think about that, until you've given pregnancy your best shot. And every month, as the doctors home in on your particular problem – and the fact that you got pregnant that one time is like the mirage on the desert that keeps you crawling with your tongue in the sand – you feel more invested: you've spent thousands and then thousands more dollars, you've got this hope-cocaine coursing through you, and all you want is to be like everyone else. Not just everyone who has a child, but everyone who's able to live their lives, to just be a person who isn't in a constant state of delayed gratification, not just because you stop drinking coffee and wine, you give up sugar and cigarettes and everything that might help you numb the pain of your wretched existence – sex, forget it, only on day 12, 14, 16, 18, and Never once you move onto the IVF because by then, who wants to? It just feels like this pointless gesture of futility. You can't even remember a time you had sex for any reason other than procreation. So…I forget where I was.

SUZANNE. Adoption.

CONNIE. Right. Well, it's hard to change courses, that's what I'm saying. It's hard to quit when there's this feeling that if you try One More Time, this whole thing will have been worth it. Especially, you know, I got so close. The one time. I was half way there, you know? So now, I feel like I'm half a mother. Half a…not widow, obviously. Though sometimes it feels like that too, since we're both half dead. But there's no word for a parent who's lost a child. And there's really not a word for a parent who's lost half a child. A child who never lived. There's no word for that at all. Just avoidance, really. Averted gazes. Awkward pauses. Cheerful suggestions to Try Again! Or Just Adopt!

(pause)

SUZANNE. Why not adopt? It's such a beautiful, spiritual thing, because we're all really one, and these boundaries – race, family, nationality, they're all so false, and evil really, this idea of Otherness is at the root of all evil –

CONNIE. You know it's not so fucking simple. To just waltz into some impoverished country and take a baby away from the only home it knows. Mr. & Mrs. Rich… WhiteMan with a big checkbook and a designer crib at home. And then you just hand the kid over to a nanny from another impoverished country so you can work twelve hours a day to pay for the fancy jogging stroller. So you can exercise when you're supposed to be spending time with the baby –

SUZANNE. Wouldn't you have a nanny anyway? I mean, wherever the baby came from –

CONNIE. But at least it's my own kid I'm ignoring. Not some sweet waif whose mother would've carried it around all day if she hadn't been murdered by marauding rebels

right in front of the baby who's going to be traumatized for the rest of her life over something she can
never even articulate.

SUZANNE. Oh my god. Connie. God.

CONNIE. I'm just saying it's not bloodless. You're taking
someone else's child.

SUZANNE. But how can you say something like that and still
feel sorry for yourself? Don't you see how lucky you are?

CONNIE. Of course I do. And that just makes it even worse.
This insanity. I know I'm insane! I just don't know how
to get better.

SUZANNE. There must be some way...

CONNIE. You act like you don't know. The only way is to
have a baby. To get pregnant and have a baby. Like
everyfuckingbodyelse on the fucking planet. God.
Don't you remember?

SUZANNE. I do remember.

CONNIE. You don't. You're too scared to remember. It's
why you can ask me all those stupid questions about
what to eat.

(SUZANNE *sighs*.)

SUZANNE. I'm sorry. It's so hard to know what someone
wants...

CONNIE. People want to be allowed to be upset. Okay?
People want to feel like you don't actually *blame* them, or
despise them for wanting something they don't have. And
for feeling desperate...loss.

SUZANNE. Some people really don't like to talk about this
sort of thing. I didn't.

CONNIE. Yes and you should be allowed to say "thank you
for caring. But I'd rather not talk about it." Wasn't it
worse – the silence?

SUZANNE. I didn't want anyone to feel sorry for me.

CONNIE. It's crazy. Everyone grieves. Everyone struggles.
And fails. Why can't we just be nice to each other
about it?

SUZANNE. You haven't failed.

CONNIE. I have. Loss is always a kind of failure. Even when someone you love dies, you feel like you failed to keep that person alive. Like somehow it's our job as humans to protect each other. To keep each other going.

SUZANNE. It is. It is our job. To keep each other going.

CONNIE. The job we're doomed to never do well enough.

(pause)

SUZANNE. But what if it seems like a friend is...stuck? Shouldn't a good friend, you know, try to...help...that person?

CONNIE. Me. You can say you mean me, I'm not an idiot.

SUZANNE. Connie, you're wasting your life.

CONNIE. I know! I know I am! But it's my life to waste!

SUZANNE. But why do I have to just sit here and say that's okay, when I don't think it is okay? I think you need to move forward.

CONNIE. Then don't be my friend if you don't like it.

SUZANNE. But my job is to keep you going. (pause) See?

(CONNIE deflates, slowly, like a blow-up doll that's been opened.)

CONNIE. I would move forward, if I could.

SUZANNE. You can.

CONNIE. How?

SUZANNE. With help.

CONNIE. I don't want to see your weird therapist.

SUZANNE. She saved my life.

CONNIE. I'm not as...mutable as you are.

SUZANNE. Just go once. Please.

(CONNIE sighs. SUZANNE reaches for her. CONNIE allows herself to be held.)

II, Scene Two

(CONNIE sits in a big armchair across from GENEVA, who is also seated, in a small room.)

GENEVA. I'm so sorry.

CONNIE. Thank you.

GENEVA. You've been through so much.

CONNIE. Yes.

GENEVA. I'd like to do a visualization with you.

CONNIE. Do we have to?

GENEVA. I think it will help.

CONNIE. Okay.

GENEVA. Uncross your arms and legs. *(CONNIE does.)* Close your eyes. *(CONNIE does. GENEVA takes a breath.)* Feel and sense a healing white light above your head. Feel and sense it falling down around and into your body, cleansing, relaxing and purifying your body as it pours in through the crown of your head, and down your spine. Let go of the muscles in your face, arms and hands…relax your internal organs, legs and feet. You are relaxed. You are cleansed. See yourself in the most beautiful place you can imagine. A place outdoors in Nature, safe, the weather is exactly how you like it to be in this place. See where the light of this place originates. Bask in it. Somewhere in this landscape your son appears to you…. Nod to me when you see him.

(After a moment, CONNIE nods.)

GENEVA. What does he want you to know?

(CONNIE shakes her head.)

He wants you to know something. What is it?

(CONNIE shakes her head.)

What does he look like? Tell me what you see.

CONNIE. Like the ultrasound. Like the negative of a tiny child. Sleeping. Beautiful. One side like me, the other like Jonas.

GENEVA. Yes. And what does he want you to know?

CONNIE. I don't know…is he angry?

GENEVA. Does he look angry?

CONNIE. No. He looks peaceful.

GENEVA. Yes. *(pause)* What does he say?

CONNIE. Nothing. He – can't talk.

GENEVA. See him. One side like you. One side like Jonas.

> *(pause)*
>
> What does he say?
>
> *(pause)*

GENEVA. It's okay. Let him speak. He wants to speak. What does he say?

CONNIE. "Let me go." *(She weeps.)* "Let me go Mommy."

GENEVA. Yes.

CONNIE. But I don't want to…

> *(***CONNIE*** *opens her eyes.)*

GENEVA. It's not by accident that these technologies exist. His spirit was here for as long as it had to be. He did what he needed to do.

CONNIE. What could he have possibly accomplished?

GENEVA. That's not for us to know.

CONNIE. He never got out! He barely had fingers! He had half a heart!

GENEVA. Maybe his intention was simply to make contact with you.

CONNIE. Why? I mean, it wasn't much contact.

GENEVA. He's touched you.

CONNIE. But in such a horrible way.

GENEVA. For now. Here's what I'm getting from him. And you tell me if this feels right to you. I'm getting that he wants you to know that he is at peace. That he only intended to come here for a short time and that he is happy. He sends you love. He wants you to let him go. Can you?

CONNIE. I don't want to.

GENEVA. Try. Close your eyes.

*(**CONNIE** closes her eyes.)*

Try to let him go.

CONNIE. I can't.

GENEVA. Try to let go.

*(**CONNIE** exhales with a shudder and a sob.)*

Good. Exhale pain. Inhale peace. Exhale pain. Inhale peace. Exhale pain.

*(As **CONNIE** continues to inhale and exhale, the sound of **SUZANNE** breathing deeply with increasing intensity rises as the lights change. **SUZANNE**'s breathing starts to sound more and more labored. She screams in pain as lights come up on **SUZANNE** and **MATT**, and **DR. MORSE** in the delivery room.)*

DR. MORSE. Here she comes! Push!

*(**SUZANNE** pushes.)*

MATT. Oh my god.

DR. MORSE. And she's here!

MATT. Oh my god.

SUZANNE. What? Is she okay?

DR. MORSE. She's great. She's perfect.

SUZANNE. *(worried)* Isn't she sweet?

MATT. She's okay....

SUZANNE. Is she okay?

DR. MORSE. She's fine.

MATT. Is she?

DR. MORSE. She's perfect.

(He hands her to a nurse.)

SUZANNE. Why do you look like that?

MATT. Is that what she's supposed to look like?

SUZANNE. Can I see her? Let me see her?

DR. MORSE. *(handing her the baby)* Look, she's beautiful.

SUZANNE. She is beautiful! Matt! She's beautiful.

MATT. ...yeah.

SUZANNE. She is! What's wrong with you?

MATT. I just didn't know she'd be so blue!

DOCTOR. Congratulations!

(SUZANNE holds the baby, ecstatic. MATT watches, overwhelmed, terrified.)

II, Scene Three

(JONAS sits on a meditation cushion, among other people, also sitting on the floor. **ALLAN KOZAN KATZ** *an American Buddhist monk with a shaved head speaks.)*

ALLAN KOZAN KATZ. Many of you have heard the story of the old fisherman who is out at dawn on a foggy day when another boat crashes into his boat, causing the water to leak into his boat. He spends the whole day cursing the careless sailor whose boat hit his then careened off into the fog without a word of apology. He works himself up into a rage that this other man is out on the water causing destruction and pain, threatening his life and livelihood. He spends the day looking for this boat that has attacked his own and finally, at the end of the day, he sees the boat and approaches it, eager to chastise the sailor. But when he gets to the offending boat, he sees that it is empty. No one was at fault. No one has offended or attacked him. Something simply happened. As soon as the fisherman realizes this, he is freed from his rage and his upset. This is like life. When we think someone or something is to blame for our suffering, or that there is even an explanation, a logic to it, we suffer more. When we can accept that there is no one in the other boat, we are free.

(Pause. **JONAS** *raises his hand.* **KOZAN** *nods at him.)*

JONAS. But what about when there is someone in the boat?

ALLAN KOZAN KATZ. There is never anyone in the boat.

JONAS. But what about when there is. When someone is driving on pain medication and they hit you. Or when someone in charge lies to a country, takes the country to war. When someone goes into a school and guns down all the children with a rifle. Shouldn't we be angry and stop these people? When there is a sailor in the boat?

ALLAN KOZAN KATZ. Even when there is a sailor in the boat, there is no sailor in the boat.

JONAS. I don't understand.

ALLAN KOZAN KATZ. What if you are both, the sailor and the empty boat? What if you are neither, the sailor nor the empty boat?

JONAS. I'm saying, I am the fisherman. And there is a sailor in the other boat. There's always a really bad, irresponsible sailor talking on their cellphone in the other boat.

ALLAN KOZAN KATZ. Is there? Are you? Next?

(**JONAS** *is annoyed.*)

II, Scene Four

(JONAS's office at the studio. MATT stops in.)

MATT. Hey.

JONAS. Hey.

MATT. I was just meeting with Nolan.

JONAS. Great! How'd it go?

MATT. I don't know...

JONAS. Well, what'd he say?

MATT. He asked me to write a few new songs to send him.

JONAS. That sounds good.

MATT. For free.

JONAS. Yeah...

MATT. I sent him like twenty songs already.

JONAS. I guess none of them are quite right.

MATT. This has been going on for months now.

JONAS. The guy's really busy.

MATT. It seems a little like a power trip. I mean, like the fact that he can put my song in the background of a scene on a TV show makes him this, like, musical genius.

JONAS. Well, he sort of is. Pop-wise.

MATT. You think?

JONAS. He's discovered some pretty great artists. I mean a lot of people have sold a lot of albums, CDs, whatever they call them now, and won a lot of Grammies they never would have if their songs hadn't been in the background of a TV show. Of this TV show.

MATT. Yeah.

(MATT picks up a little robot on Jonas' desk and winds it up.)

JONAS. So are you going to write the new songs?

MATT. I don't know. It doesn't really work for me like that.

JONAS. What do you mean? Why not?

MATT. Just, you know, that's not really my process. To try to come up with what someone else wants.

JONAS. Then don't do it.

MATT. Yeah.

(**MATT** *lets the robot loose on Jonas' desk.*)

JONAS. And stop complaining about your life.

MATT. I don't complain about my life. (**JONAS** *snorts.*) Any more than you do.

JONAS. Well, I have more to complain about, don't you think?

MATT. Are you kidding me?

JONAS. Are you kidding me?!

MATT. I mean, I know you guys have had some trouble –

JONAS. Some trouble.

MATT. A really bad loss. But there's so much you have, that like, a fraction of people on the planet have.

JONAS. It's okay. We don't need to talk about this.

MATT. We do – I think we should.

JONAS. No, we really shouldn't.

MATT. We had losses too you know.

JONAS. And when you did, you felt like I do now.

MATT. Yeah, but I was wrong.

JONAS. Well, it's easy to say now, isn't it?

MATT. That's why I'm saying it. To help you.

JONAS. I don't want your help. Help yourself. Feel good about what you have.

MATT. I do.

JONAS. You just came in here and complained about the best opportunity you've had in years! That I got for you, actually. I mean, fuck.

MATT. I thanked you.

JONAS. You didn't actually. But that's not even the point.

MATT. I'm just not sure I can come up with –

JONAS. All you do is bitch about how you can't afford to fix your roof!

MATT. I'm not like you. I don't want to do a version of what I do. I want to do what I really do, or not do it all. Everyone else is doing approximations of the truth. Why should I?

JONAS. So you can fix your roof. So you can feed your kid you tried so hard to get.

MATT. Well, it was Suzanne, really, who wanted her.

JONAS. So now you don't want your daughter?

MATT. No, it's not that. It's just...now I feel like I have to fix the fucking roof.

JONAS. Yes. Exactly. You have to grow up.

MATT. But don't all the grown-ups seem really...depressing? I mean, have you been to a playground, lately?

JONAS. No. Matt. I haven't.

MATT. All the parents. They look like total shit, man. And they have nothing to say. When you try to talk to them, they tell you how many hours their kid slept last night. And the night before. And the night before that. Like that's a conversation. And they all have these deranged looks in their eye. Screaming "Good job! Good job!" every time the kid comes down the slide, or drinks from his stupid sippy cup. And dude, the words that come out of your mouth – "binky?" "burpie?" "diapie?" "She had a big poopy!" That's, like, the most dramatic event of my day.

JONAS. It's better than when your own poop was the most dramatic event your day.

MATT. Yeah, well. It wasn't. *(pause)* My mom used to always say "it's different when they're yours" but I can see these parents are bored out of their minds. They're in a coma, man. And so was my mother, actually. It wasn't different for her. She had to be on barbiturates to make it through a day at the park.

JONAS. So maybe you guys should kill baby Ella.

MATT. And everyone spends their whole pregnancy coming up with a perfect retro name, like that's going to make the whole family incredibly cool, and then it turns out we all came up with same five names. Suzanne almost lost her mind when she found out how many Ellas there are in our neighborhood. She went to this New Mother's group, which is another place you should avoid if you ever want to have an erection again in your life, and there were like six hundred baby Ellas. I thought she was going to just gun them all down. She's a total bitch because she's so tired and fat and there's no time to paint. It's just, it's kind of a drag over there.

JONAS. So, what are you saying? You regret it? You regret having a child?

MATT. No. *(pause)* I think that might be psychologically impossible. Like regretting being toilet trained or something.

JONAS. A lot of people abandon their children.

MATT. Well, yeah, that I understand. Feeling like you can't deal with taking care of them. Like there's got to be someone else who can do a better job. Anyone, maybe. But I doubt anyone regrets having a child. They just regret…becoming a parent. I love Ella. I just hate her parents.

(pause)

JONAS. I'm not sure, are you asking for sympathy?

MATT. I'm just saying, everything you want – once you get it, it's not…it's never what you thought it would be.

JONAS. I wouldn't know.

MATT. Sure you would. Is having money everything you wanted it to be?

JONAS. I never wanted to have money, particularly.

MATT. Then why do you?

JONAS. I just wanted to do what I do.

MATT. Right. But you don't do what you do. You do a version of it that makes money. So, obviously, you want to make money.

JONAS. I want to be able to fix my roof.

MATT. I'm just saying, I read this article, they did all these studies about happiness and they found out that people with kids are actually less happy than people without kids. But the people with kids *think* they're happier than they used to be, because they're like heroin addicts? Their world gets so small, all they have is the drug, the kid, so the brain translates it as – my kids make me so happy. But really, it's because the kids are *all* they have. They don't go to clubs or to movies, or do anything that used to give them pleasure.

JONAS. When was the last time you derived pleasure from a movie?

MATT. Well, whatever it was you enjoyed…

JONAS. I don't enjoy anything anymore.

MATT. What about –

JONAS. Nothing. Trust me. Food. Sex. Trees. The ocean. My health, even. None of it has any…impact.

MATT. Well how do you know a baby's going to have an impact?

JONAS. I don't. *(pause)* Maybe it won't. Maybe I've gotten so used to this feeling of…deprivation that no matter what I have, I'll always feel it's not enough.

MATT. That's the human condition, dude. That's what I'm saying.

JONAS. It didn't used to be. For me. I used to really feel it was enough, just to have my cup of coffee in the morning. The light on the leaves of the tree outside my bedroom window…. Even when I was going off to some shitty job, waiting tables, or selling shoes, just having my life, you know? It was…enough.

MATT. In retrospect. I'm sure at the time you wanted more.

JONAS. But even wanting more was…sweet then.

MATT. When you're young, wanting more is fun. Because you think you're going to get it. Your whole life is basically foreplay. Or like looking to score drugs. You know it's going to happen, you just don't know when.

JONAS. And now you know it's not going to happen. You're never going to be any better than you are. No matter what changes.

MATT. That's what I'm saying man. So it's like, why fix the roof? Or write the lame song? Why have a kid, even, you know?

JONAS. Because you need something. To move you forward. God, you need some fucking thing to get you through the hours of sitting in traffic watching everything that was ever beautiful slowly disappear from the planet. You need to feel you are, in some way, making something good, something or someone that could bring some small spark of joy into the horror.

MATT. Maybe. But maybe that's just what you tell yourself. To justify the constant need for something new. Not beautiful, or joyous, or whatever, just, you know, different. But nothing is ever really better than it was before.

(pause)

JONAS. Some things are. Marriage was.

MATT. Marriage.

JONAS. Not, getting married.

MATT. Yeah, cause that kind of sucks.

JONAS. But having someone I wanted to...be with that much. I mean, I liked being alone. But then...it was so much...better...to be together. And Connie wanted to get married, so I just went along with the whole thing, but then, for some reason, when we were picking out our rings, we found the band we both liked, and as soon as I put it on, I felt like, yes, I want to be married.

MATT. It's a nice ring, man.

JONAS. It sounds so insane. Like I was transformed by an accessory. Or like a fairy tale or something. But it was a sort of metamorphosis from being a single...organism to part of a larger...society, actually. It was an expansion, to...include this other person. And then we got pregnant and expanded again – we included our baby. And then we lost him. And then I lost her. And now I'm like a little town that's been abandoned.

*(Pause. **JONAS** wipes his eyes.)*

MATT. But you and Connie, you're not...?

JONAS. No, we're together. We're just not...together.

MATT. I'm sorry, man.

JONAS. So, yeah. It's not about wanting what I don't have. It's about wanting it back – what I did have. *(pause)* The whole reason I stayed alone all those years was so I wouldn't have to feel anything like what I feel now. And part of me is like, why? Why couldn't I have just... continued on as I was?

MATT. Because that's not life, dude. Living without love –

JONAS. I had love. I had friends –

MATT. Living without the kind of love that scares the shit out of you, I'm saying.

JONAS. You don't want it. I mean, all this crap about being old or missing your old stupid life – and your life wasn't that great before, I hate to remind you. You're no more boring now than you were then. It's all just fear. Of feeling like I do right now. You'd rather despise your family than love them so much that losing them would be an annihilation. Of who you became when they...joined you.

(A long emotional silence.)

MATT. Fuck you, man.

JONAS. Yeah, yeah, yeah. Just fix the roof.

*(**MATT** puts the robot on Jonas' desk. They both watch it as it marches across the desk and plunges over the side.)*

II, Scene Five

(**MATT** *sings.*)

MATT. I fixed the roof. Between you and the sky
I paid the man to make sure you stay dry.
Now when the sky tears open
And falls down on us

The rain taps on the tin
I got all these walls surrounding us
I won't let anyone in.

When it was just two of us inside
We had so much less to hide away.

(*The baby wails.* **SUZANNE** *calls.*)

SUZANNE (*O.S.*) Matt! Shut up!

(**MATT** *writes down a chord.*)

MATT. Less to hide away.

SUZANNE (*O.S.*) MATT!!

MATT. Sorry! (*then, playing more quietly.*) Now it feels safe, to sleep here, little girl –

(*Harried,* **SUZANNE** *comes out, holding a tightly swaddled baby.*)

SUZANNE. She hates it when you play.

MATT. You say that, but I don't think it's true.

SUZANNE. Well she cries when you play and smiles when you stop. What do you think?

MATT. I think she has gas.

SUZANNE. Look. She's smiling. Because you stopped.

(**MATT** *picks up the guitar and plays a few chords. The baby starts to wail.*)

MATT. What kind of baby doesn't want to her father sing?

SUZANNE. A very sick baby. Our baby.

(**SUZANNE** *hands him the baby.*)

MATT. It's crazy. I wrote this song for her!

SUZANNE. You wrote it for NBC.

MATT. And for her.

SUZANNE. Well let's hope NBC likes it better than she does. *(She starts to go.)* If I don't lie down right now, I'll go insane.

MATT. Did you feed her?

SUZANNE. She's not hungry.

MATT. Did you try?

SUZANNE. How else would I know she's not hungry?

MATT. When?

SUZANNE. Recently.

(She turns to go.)

MATT. I think you should try again before you go.

SUZANNE. Matt. She's not. Hungry.

MATT. Did you give her her paci?

SUZANNE. She doesn't want it.

MATT. Because she's hungry.

SUZANNE. She's not fucking hungry.

MATT. Well, why is she crying?

SUZANNE. She's sick of me. She needs to get some space from me right now. She misses you.

(The baby cries.)

MATT. She's still crying. And here I am. Not playing.

*(**MATT** rocks the baby.)*

SUZANNE. She can smell me. She wants you to herself. She's competitive.

MATT. Let me just –

*(He brings the baby to **SUZANNE**'s breast.)*

SUZANNE. What are you doing?

*(**SUZANNE** starts to move away. **MATT** grabs her arm and pulls open her shirt. **SUZANNE** squirms.)*

Matt! Jesus!

MATT. Let me just see how she reacts.

(He puts the baby's face at **SUZANNE**'s *breast.)*

SUZANNE. Ow.

(The baby is drinking.)

MATT. Look. She's starved. She's totally starving.

*(***SUZANNE** *takes the baby.)*

SUZANNE. This is so manipulative, baby!

MATT. She's not manipulative. She's an infant.

SUZANNE. I swear to god. She would not have anything to do with this breast when we were inside.

MATT. Maybe she just needed some air.

*(***SUZANNE** *starts crying.)*

Suze?

SUZANNE. I can't take it.

MATT. You're tired.

SUZANNE. I haven't made anything new in months.

MATT. You made a person.

SUZANNE. That's true. But I can't sell her.

MATT. We could get a lot for her.

SUZANNE. *(to the baby)* I'm sorry. Mommy doesn't really want to sell you. Even when you're a manipulative bitch.

*(***MATT** *picks up his guitar. He plays the tune he was working out before. The baby eats.)*

MATT. See? She likes it.

SUZANNE. Is it new?

MATT. Will you hate me if it is?

SUZANNE. Yes. Of course. I'll hate you even if it isn't.

MATT. Why?

SUZANNE. I don't know. You look so free.

MATT. Free? How am I free?

SUZANNE. You could go. Any time. You could always just… go.

MATT. So could you.

SUZANNE. I can't. I belong to someone.

MATT. Don't I?

SUZANNE. Not as irrevocably.

MATT. I'm not planning to go anywhere.

SUZANNE. I just mean you can walk out the door…for any length of time. An hour, a week, forever…

MATT. You're really tired.

SUZANNE. Really. How can you tell? God, I used to be this passionate "emerging" artist. This unique point of view.

MATT. Baby. Come on. It's a transition…

SUZANNE. That journalist came to my studio and not only did I have to dig out paintings from last year, but I couldn't even remember why I made them or what any of my work is about.

MATT. You're just not used to –

SUZANNE. All those women who say they have time for everything once baby comes, they just get more organized – they have nannies! Those bitches! Of course there's enough time, if you have a STAFF!

MATT. I'm writing this for NBC, Suze.

SUZANNE. I wasn't –

MATT. Yes you were.

SUZANNE. Sorry. I'd be happy to work. If I could. God. I'd be thrilled to churn out a hundred pretty landscapes, to just disappear into my studio for hours and get drenched in toxic chemicals –

MATT. Then do it. Go back to work. I'll take care of her.

SUZANNE. How am I going to give you my breasts?

MATT. You work in the garage. It's not that far a trip.

SUZANNE. I know, but then I have to stop and get cleaned up, then come back out – it's impossible to get into a flow.

MATT. She takes a bottle half the time.

SUZANNE. Once a day. Once. Out of six hundred feedings a day.

MATT. She takes a bottle. So go drown in toxic chemicals and I'll take care of the baby.

SUZANNE. You'll take care of her.

MATT. Yes.

SUZANNE. What about at night?

MATT. I get up.

SUZANNE. You say "the baby" and go back to sleep.

MATT. That is so untrue. I've walked with her. I know how she operates. I knew she was hungry –

SUZANNE. Yeah, but the relentlessness of it...

MATT. She's less relentless than you are. Bitching about it all the time.

SUZANNE. That's nice.

MATT. Sorry.

(**SUZANNE** *hands the baby to* **MATT**.)

SUZANNE. Enjoy.

(*She heads out.*)

MATT. Where are you going?

SUZANNE. Out. To see if there's still life on the planet.

MATT. You're in your underwear!

SUZANNE. None of my clothes fit me anyway!

MATT. Do we have any bottles?

SUZANNE. In the fridge, Daddy!

(**SUZANNE** *walks out in her nightgown.* **MATT** *picks up his guitar and plays. The baby cries.*)

II, Scene Six

(**CONNIE** *sits on the floor surrounded by books and papers.* **JONAS** *comes in.*)

JONAS. What is this? *(He picks up a book.)* "The Ultimate Insiders Guide to Adoption" *(another)* "International Adoption. Making it Work for You." Okay.

CONNIE. I think we should adopt someone.

JONAS. Okay.

CONNIE. What do you think?

(pause)

JONAS. I don't know.

CONNIE. You don't?

JONAS. I mean, conceptually, it's...nice. But...I don't know.

CONNIE. Why not? What don't you know?

JONAS. I just...I don't want to want anyone. Else. Anymore.

CONNIE. What do you mean? You don't want a baby now?

JONAS. I'd be happy if a baby showed up. If someone just came to the door with a baby, that would be fine. If it just happened like that – someone came along who needed me. Us.

CONNIE. Well there are thousands of children who need us.

JONAS. In theory. I just don't want to do anything to get them.

CONNIE. You don't have to. I'll do everything. You just show up to the home visit wearing a tie. And act...nurturing. For an hour.

JONAS. I just...yeah, it doesn't feel right. For me. Right now.

CONNIE. Why not? Because it won't feel like it's yours?

JONAS. No, I'm sure it'd feel like mine. Once it got here.

CONNIE. Because they will, even if you don't feel it right away –

JONAS. I just really don't want to convince someone to give me a baby.

CONNIE. I'll convince them. And we don't have to do it domestically, selling ourselves to some birth mother –

JONAS. I'd rather die.

CONNIE. We just fill out a bunch of forms and write an essay – I'll write yours if you want, and then we just wait a few months in some cases, but eventually, a baby shows up. Some countries bring them to you. They practically do just show up at your door.

JONAS. Yeah…

CONNIE. What?

JONAS. I can't.

CONNIE. WHY NOT?

JONAS. I can't ask someone to give me a child. I just feel like, what kind of crazed lunatic would put a child in this home?

CONNIE. This home is not that bad. For a neglected orphan from some impoverished country? This home would be like heaven.

JONAS. Would it? I don't know. I might rather be in an orphanage.

(Silence. **CONNIE** *tears up.)*

CONNIE. That's horrible.

JONAS. I'm sorry. It's just the atmosphere. Of desperation.

CONNIE. An orphanage is a lot more desperate. These babies just sit in their cribs for days with no one holding them!

JONAS. Isn't that how it feels here?

CONNIE. That's in such poor taste.

JONAS. I know we have a pool, Connie. I'm just saying, despite your many pairs of shoes, don't you feel like you're sitting alone in your crib?

(silence)

CONNIE. It's still shoes and a pool.

JONAS. It's not enough for you, so why should it be enough for a child?

CONNIE. Because a child would make it enough. A child would make it everything.

JONAS. I don't know.

CONNIE. Trust me.

JONAS. I'm saying. I don't want to think about this anymore.

CONNIE. How can we not think about it?

JONAS. I can. I can not think about it.

CONNIE. Well I can't.

JONAS. I'm not asking you not to. I'm just asking you to understand that I can't.

CONNIE. So what am I supposed to do?

JONAS. I don't know. That's up to you.

(**CONNIE** *bursts into tears.* **JONAS** *is frozen.*)

CONNIE. I can't believe you're not going to let me do the only thing that could possibly make me feel better!

JONAS. I didn't say I wasn't going to let you.

CONNIE. Well, what am I supposed to do? We're fucking married.

JONAS. I'm just so tired of…not-having…ness.

CONNIE. Me too! That's what I'm saying.

JONAS. But adoption, it's just more of that.

CONNIE. It's not though. It's havingness!

JONAS. Not until it is.

CONNIE. But it will be. It's inevitable.

JONAS. Nothing is inevitable.

CONNIE. International adoption is inevitable.

JONAS. What about what happened to Jenny?

CONNIE. So we won't adopt from Romania.

JONAS. Or China now, I heard.

CONNIE. Korea, then. Guatemala. There are babies all over the world who need homes.

JONAS. I'm just saying, nothing is sure. Something can always go wrong.

CONNIE. Something can always go wrong sitting here in the living room. A plane could crash through the roof.

JONAS. Yes, but then it just happened. It's not something we sought out.

CONNIE. This is very bizarre. What's wrong with you?

JONAS. I need to find a way to feel happy with what we have, what I have, before I can ask for something more. Something else. *(pause)* Because there's always something more you can need. More you will need. If you can't be happy with what you have now.

CONNIE. Okay. Normally, I mean on any other subject, I would agree with you. But this thing, a baby, it's a genetic mandate, it's biological. It's every cell in my being, screaming. Half way transformed, like…is there a mythological figure who gets stuck halfway through a transformation? Like those Rodin statues? Where the figures are half stone, half human.

JONAS. I don't know.

CONNIE. Let's look it up.

JONAS. I don't want to look it up.

*(**CONNIE** goes to the computer)*

JONAS. Let's please, not, look it up.

CONNIE. I have to. I have to. *(typing)* "Myth. Half transformed."

JONAS. You'll never get it that way.

CONNIE. *(reading)* "Shape-shifters, werewolves?" Maybe it is like being a werewolf. Half man, half wolf. Half mother, half…?

JONAS. Wolf.

CONNIE. Yes. Half-starved for blood.

JONAS. That sounds right.

CONNIE. That's how it feels. This primeval, violent, hunger.

(She types.)

"Werewolf." *(reading)* "a person who shapeshifts into a wolf or wolflike creature." That's me. "…for the sake of sating a craving for human flesh." I have a craving for human flesh.

JONAS. Totally.

CONNIE. It's not the same as wanting a better job, or a bigger house. It's the most basic human drive.

JONAS. Love.

CONNIE. Yes, it's Love –

JONAS. No, I'm saying Love is the most basic human drive.

CONNIE. Well, it's semantics, isn't it?

JONAS. No. A lot of people don't reproduce – don't need to reproduce. They have love in other ways –

CONNIE. I know, I used to be that person. Before I became a werewolf…statue. *(pause)* I just wanted…you.

JONAS. I know. I remember.

(A sad pause. She reaches for him. He hesitates. There is a knock at the door.)

CONNIE. Messenger?

JONAS. Are you waiting for something?

CONNIE. There's always something that could be coming.

(JONAS goes to the door. Still in her nightgown, SUZANNE walks in.)

SUZANNE. I left Matt.

CONNIE. What do you mean?

SUZANNE. I just…walked out.

JONAS. Did you have a fight?

SUZANNE. I don't know. I guess. I just had to get out of there.

CONNIE. Where's Ella?

SUZANNE. We don't call her that anymore.

CONNIE. You don't.

SUZANNE. She needs a new name.

CONNIE. What are you talking about?

SUZANNE. I can't make the same mistake twice. I'm waiting until I really know what's out there. For now, she's just Baby.

JONAS. You didn't leave her with Matt.

SUZANNE. He's not going to eat her.

(Pause. She sits down.)

Your house is so neat. Everything in it's place.

CONNIE. It's Jonas. He cleans when he's upset.

JONAS. So the house has been immaculate for years now.

CONNIE. What if she gets hungry?

SUZANNE. I know, I'm starving.

CONNIE. The baby. What if she gets hungry?

SUZANNE. There's milk.

JONAS. Are you having post-partum depression?

SUZANNE. No. I just hate being a mother. It turns out.

(CONNIE glares at her.)

JONAS. It's just the hormones.

SUZANNE. I don't think so. Unless Matt has hormones too. I think we just…no one warned us we might not, you know, enjoy the experience.

CONNIE. Why are you saying this?

SUZANNE. I wanted you to know. Your life is perfect as it is.

JONAS. Exactly.

CONNIE. Oh please.

SUZANNE. Look around you! Look at this house! At your husband! Do you know how many men are like him? Like five on the planet! Your work – you're one of the most successful women in your field.

CONNIE. For now. I think it's a liability that I no longer give a fuck.

SUZANNE. But look at what you do have –

CONNIE. You want it? Give me the baby and you can have my house and my bank account. All my assets. I'll take your kid and your paint…sets. *(pause)* If this was one of my stupid movies there'd be some tinkling music right now and suddenly I'd be wearing that ratty nightgown. You'd be in Marc Jacobs. Then in the end, we'd both learn a meaningful lesson.

SUZANNE. I could use a meaningful lesson.

CONNIE. No one really wants a meaningful lesson. They just want confirmation of what they already believe.

JONAS. We just want to feel less alone. Isn't that a more compassionate way to see it?

SUZANNE. Yes. Thank you.

CONNIE. But isn't it all just a lie? We are alone. That's the reality.

SUZANNE. Oh, God. That is the reality.

JONAS. It's only half the reality. We're alone, and we're not.

CONNIE. But even when we're not, we are.

JONAS. Even when we are, we're not.

CONNIE. Jonas has gotten really into Zen.

SUZANNE. I've got to start meditating.

(The bell rings.)

JONAS. Matt?

(The sound of a baby crying.)

SUZANNE. And that fucking baby.

(JONAS opens the door. MATT walks in, desperately bouncing the baby.)

JONAS. Hi.

MATT. Is she here?

(JONAS steps aside, MATT walks in. And tries to thrust the baby into SUZANNE's arms. She steps back. The baby continues to cry in MATT's arms.)

SUZANNE. I thought you knew how she operated.

MATT. Do you not have a maternal bone in your body? Look at her.

SUZANNE. It's not good.

MATT. She's traumatized.

SUZANNE. So am I.

JONAS. She's not traumatized.

CONNIE. She's just upset.

(JONAS grabs the baby and soothes her. CONNIE creeps over to JONAS' side and strokes the baby's face.)

JONAS. It's okay. It's okay.

CONNIE. Poor little thing.

(SUZANNE *lies down on the couch and closes her eyes. The baby quiets down.*)

JONAS. See? She's fine.

CONNIE. She just needs some love.

SUZANNE. It's so quiet here. And so cool. The trees.

JONAS. Look at that face. That's some sweet face.

CONNIE. Let me hold her.

(*She takes the baby.* MATT *goes to look at Suzanne's painting that is hanging on the wall. It's the red one from the first scene.*)

MATT. That's a really nice painting...

(*Lights fade on* CONNIE, JONAS *and the baby,* SUZANNE, MATT *and the painting.*)

End of Play

From the Reviews of
WHAT THEY HAVE...

"Bottom Line: Kate Robin's comic triumph is a kindler, gentler *Who's Afraid of Virginia Woolf* for the 21st century...consistently and often brilliantly funny...draws on an impressive range of associations that leaves you thinking once the laughter wears off...it may have you leaving the theater with an inspiring new perspective on your life, your relationships and the way you interact with the world around you."
- *Hollywood Reporter*

"Ms. Robin wrote for HBO's popular *Six Feet Under*...she can produce reams of chatty, entertaining dialogue for characters that audiences will find cozily familiar. *What They Have* is also sensitive and smart in its analysis of the shifting emotional dynamics both between couples and within them...marked by a sincerity and a probing honesty about the way people live today."
- The *New York Times*

"A realistic, intelligent, heartfelt and heartbreaking look at two very different couples living in modern Hollywood...this is one of the best plays of the year...*What They Have* will become the must-have script for theaters across the country."
- TheaterMania.com

"Kate Robin's sweetly bleak meditation on parenthood, jealousy and compromise...whose strength of ideas keep coming back to me again and again, days after I've seen it. That's something rare and beautiful in the theater."
- *OCWeekly*

Also by
Kate Robin...

Anon

ANON

Kate Robin

2m, 12f / Drama / Areas

Anon. follows two couples as they cope with sexual addiction. Trip and Allison are young and healthy, but he's more interested in his abnormally large porn collection than in her. While they begin to work through both of their own sexual and relationship hang-ups, Trip's parents are stuck in the roles they've been carving out for years in their dysfunctional marriage. In between scenes with these four characters, 10 different women, members of a support group for those involved with individuals with sex addiction issues, tell their stories in monologues that are alternately funny and harrowing..

In addition to *Anon.*, Robin's play *What They Have* was also commissioned by South Coast Repertory. Her plays have also been developed at Manhattan Theater Club, Playwrights Horizons, New York Theatre Workshop, The Eugene O'Neill Theater Center's National Playwrights Conference, JAW/West at Portland Center Stage and Ensemble Studio Theatre. Television and film credits include "*Six Feet Under*" (writer/supervising producer) and "*Coming Soon.*" Robin received the 2003 Princess Grace Statuette for playwriting and is an alumna of New Dramatists.

OTHER TITLES AVAILABLE FROM SAMUEL FRENCH

SMUDGE

Rachel Axler

2m, 1f / Dark Comedy / Interior

A dark comedy about the changing face of the American family and the limits of love and cheesecake, as a hopeful young couple gives birth to a smudge, written by two-time Emmy Award winner Rachel Axler.

"For signs of intelligent life in the theatrical universe, I hereby refer you to *Smudge*, Rachel Axler's pitch-black comedy."
- Marilyn Stasio, *Variety*

"Creepy and funny. Precise and imaginative. Parenthood never looked weirder or more terrifying than it does in *Smudge*"
- Rachel Saltz, *The New York Times*

"The mysterious newborn in Rachel Axler's smart, piquant Smudge is not lovable-looking... In some sense, Axler's dark comedy is a horror story: a parent's nightmare rendered with sometimes lyrical surrealism.... A meditation on ambiguity and ambivalence, *Smudge* also illustrates ambition: a parent's, thwarted, and a playwright's, achieved."
- Adam Feldman, *Time Out New York*

"*Smudge* is filled with laughs, due to Rachel Axler's tart way with quips, director Pam MacKinnon's brisk, unsentimental touch, and the ability of both Greg Keller and Cassie Beck to make their characters real and complex."
- Jennifer Farrar, *Associated Press*

"An ambitious play, one that ponders such big questions as how to communicate and what it means to be alive. A play that sticks with you, both for its laughs and for its message."
- Julia Furay, *CurtainUp*